ENTICED BY THE CORSAIR

No one likes a rebellious captive.

I learned that the hard way. I've been abducted from earth and cruelly tormented for my fighting spirit until I learned that the only thing that would keep me safe is to be sweet and calm and agreeable. It's what keeps me alive.

When I'm rescued by space pirates, they tell me I'm safe. I'm told I can be myself again, get as angry as I want, laugh and cry and scream all I need. I don't believe them, of course. I certainly don't believe Alyvos, the 'muscle' of the pirate ship. Everyone says that he likes nothing more than a good fight, but to me, he's kind and protective. How can I fear someone who holds me tenderly through the night and has fuzzy skin?

But my pirate wants more from me than I'm ready to give. He wants my fiery spirit...and I'm not sure it's there anymore.

ENTICED BY THE CORSAIR

CORSAIRS — BOOK THREE

RUBY DIXON

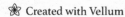

ALYVOS

I crack my knuckles as I watch the table across the cantina.

"I don't like this," Tarekh says at my side. Of course, he's been saying that ever since the plan was agreed upon. Male's like a broken voice-comm, stuck on a permanent loop.

"It'll be fine," I tell him for the hundredth time in the last hour. "Cat was good with the plan."

"Yes, but I'm not good with it," Tarekh growls. He fingers the gun holstered at his hip. "I'm not good with this at all."

I should probably say something to reassure him. Sentorr would. Kivian would. Fran sure would. But all I do is crack my knuckles again, the blood singing in my veins at the thought of the upcoming fight. Some would say it's a nervous habit, except I'm not nervous. I'm full of anticipation and irrational anger, both of which make my bloodthirsty pulse beat harder with every passing moment.

I'm the wrong one to calm Tarekh down as his mate is fake-bartered away.

Across the room, Cat wails and looks distraught, plucking at the device around her neck. She's seated on the floor at Kivian's feet, a chain and collar standing out against her pale skin and the slinky costume she's wearing. Kivian stares at the gambling table before him and looks almost as worried as the human, which is good. It means they're selling it hard, and right now, the szzt pirates across from them are buying it.

I'll say one thing for Cat. She's as good an actor as Kivian is. Her tears look real and terrified. No wonder it's making Tarekh crazy. I nudge my buddy with my elbow. "You know she's fine with the plan. Kef it all, it was her plan."

"I know," Tarekh snarls again, but he doesn't sound pleased. He sounds like he's strangling on the words. A glance over at him shows his jaw is clenched so tight I'm surprised his fangs don't snap off. I don't know why he's so upset. Things are going exactly as we hoped.

At the last station we were at, we heard about a few szzt pirates hanging out at Rakhar IV who had a taste for human females and had acquired a stolen shipment of plas-guns that were supposed to go to a colony three systems over. They're selling the guns to the highest bidder, and right now the ooli are interested.

I keffing hate the ooli, not just because they sided with the Threshians in the war. I hate their faces and their smug attitudes, like mesakkah are primitive idiots just because we've got horns and plated skin instead of the squishy damp surface of their own bodies. Because our brains are slightly smaller than an ooli's brain matter.

But mostly because they sided with the Threshians in the war, let's be honest.

We were all on board with stealing the guns from them. Two loudmouth szzt who were telling everyone on the station that they had expensive contraband weaponry? They're just begging to have it stolen from them. If not by us, then by someone else. Seems a shame to let all that money slip away, so we decided to hatch a plan. And so far it's working perfectly.

Kivian would do his foolish song and dance, pretending to be a petty outer-rim lordling instead of the pirate he is. He'd show up in his gaudiest clothing with his human pet at his side, lose badly at sticks, and lose Cat to them. Once she's on their ship, Cat'll override their shields with a chip that Sentorr made for her and we've trained her how to use. She knows where to insert it in their ship's circuitry and how to activate it. She's got the thing tucked into her mouth right now, and she's got weapons stashed all over her flimsy little costume. Even the collar she's wearing is reverse-engineered so she can shock other people with it instead of it being used against her. The pale flesh she's showing has been coated with a reagent that will make her captors sleepy and unable to get their cocks erect. She's in no danger. Once she gets on board, she'll put them to sleep and then we take over their ship, disable it, politely lift the goods, and then go on our way. It's a simple plan, made all the more beautiful because it's their own greedy foolishness that'll get these szzt into trouble.

I love it. I wish I had more heads to break, but it's still a good plan and I like the idea of taking guns from the Threshians. Plus, I'm hoping the szzt give us a fight and refuse to come calmly. That'll let me work off some nervous energy.

I shift on my feet, cracking my knuckles again as I watch Cat weep copious tears. The lead of her chain is handed over to one avid-looking szzt male. Kivian leans back in his chair, looking for all the world as if he's surprised that he's managed to lose at sticks. Cat jerks on the chain, protesting, and one of the szzt grabs her jaw in its clawed grip, making her go still.

Tarekh starts forward.

This is exactly what I'm here to prevent. A bar brawl might be my favorite thing in the world, but right now it'd serve no purpose. I grab Tarekh and jerk him backward before he charges into the cantina and gives away that we're Kivian's crew and not just a couple of drinkers hiding out in a corner. "Don't. This is exactly what is supposed to happen. We'll get to knock heads later."

The medic's eyes widen at me, his nostrils flaring, and for a moment, I think that the only fight I'm going to get tonight is the one Tarekh's going to give me. There's murderous rage in his eyes, and I give him a gleeful smile, baring my own fangs. Daring him to attack.

Just one good punch. That's the only excuse I need. Tarekh's my friend, but I'll welcome any chance to use my fists, any opportunity to get some of this rage out of my head.

"Can you two quit your dick-swinging for five minutes?" Fran's voice pipes into the comm chip hidden in the shell of my ear. "Kivian's getting up from the table. Lay low and we watch to make sure they take Cat back to their ship."

I grin at Tarekh with unholy glee, daring him to take a swing at me anyhow. I'm itching for a good fight. Any fight. "Do it," I taunt him.

He snorts and turns away from me, his gaze searching the cantina. His body tenses. "They're taking her away."

"And they're headed in the direction of the szzt ship, so that's a good sign," Fran chimes in. "All right. I'll tell Kivian to change out of his fancypants gear and into something that can take a few splatters of blood. You two get into position. Sentorr's got the ship fueled and ready to go at a moment's notice."

"I can speak for myself," Sentorr says drily into the comm. He sounds as stuffy as ever, and I know it bothers him that not only is Fran crew now, but she's helping out in jobs. He really hates that. I guess it's different when the females are just bedwarmers. Me, I appreciate a good feisty female. Cat and Fran have slowly won me over because they're the most stubborn, irritating, headstrong females I've ever met, human or no. Sentorr's still coming around. Even now, his voice sounds frosty. "But yes, as the human said, we're fueled."

I nod at nothing in particular. "We'll follow behind, then."

After all, maybe Cat will fight the szzt in the halls to the docking bay and we'll get to fight anyhow.

WE FOLLOW down the twisty passages of the station. Rakhar IV has musty-smelling recycled air that makes my nose twitch, but I don't complain. Even the stink of this place is better than others I've experienced. Nothing's as bad as the atmosphere on Thresh II, and on bad days, I wake up smelling it coming out of my pores, as if I'm still there, dug down in a terraforming trench, waiting for a rescue ship that never comes. But then again, I always connect everything back to Thresh II, even though it's been years and years since I saw that ugly keffing planet.

Some things you just never forget.

It's quiet as Tarekh and I approach the docking bay that the szzt are occupying. Their ship's a small junker, the outside deceivingly bland and unassuming. Those are the best kinds of ships to pirate in. Just look at ours. *The Lovesick Fool* has a ridiculous name and a benign appearance. We're not sleek like a planetary racer. We're not armored like a war vessel or covered in guns. Least, not as far as most can tell. Tarekh, Sentorr and I have spent years modifying the ship for that specific appearance. So it doesn't surprise me to see that the szzt's *Bringer of Many Joys* is nondescript.

There's no sign of Cat and her captors, but the engines are humming, as if prepping to take off. "Looks like they've boarded," I tell Tarekh.

He makes a strangled sound in his throat, and I know this is difficult for him. "Let's get on the *Fool* so we can follow them."

We head back to the *Fool*, which is docked a few bays over. Tarekh immediately heads for the bridge, no doubt so he can watch Sentorr monitor Cat's vitals and position on ship through the injectable device placed under the skin of one underarm. Me, I stay by the hatch even when we dock and start cruising away from the station. I wouldn't be able to sit anyhow. I'm too keyed up. Too ready to fight. I mentally go through my weapons over and over again. There's a knife at my hip, but I rarely use it. Ends a fight too quick. Same with my blaster that's holstered at my belt. Can't use that today because the junker they're using is an older class and not blaster-proof. So it's knives or fists. I prefer to use my fists and I pull on my favorite gloves, the ones with reinforced metal over the knuckles so my hits can hurt more. I flex my hands, pleased. This is—

"Get me the fuck out of here!"

Cat's voice hisses over the comm, cutting through my thoughts.

I straighten and push away from the wall, frowning. The plan was to follow the others deeper into space, far away from Rakhar IV —or far enough that the disabled, drifting junker wouldn't be found by authorities until we were well out of the system. Cat hasn't been on their ship long enough for the station to be out of sight.

"Cat? Love, tell me what's wrong," Tarekh immediately responds, and I can hear the tension through the comm. Ten credits says he's practically shoved Sentorr away from his control panels in his effort to try to "help" his mate.

"This place is not cool! Not at all! I need you to come get me. Now!" Her voice rises a hysterical note. "They left me in the cargo bay and put me in a cage and it's dark—"

"We should have sent her with a flashlight," someone murmurs. Fran.

"—And no, the dark is fine. But like...I can smell meat! Dead things! Lots of dead things! And I am freaking the fuck out!" Her voice catches. "So please, please. Come and get me. I don't care if we get this job. I can't do this. I can't—"

"We're coming," Tarekh says firmly.

"Now hold on," Kivian protests. "We're far too close—"

"We're coming," Tarekh repeats. "It's keffing final. I'm coming for you, baby. Just find a wall and put your back to it."

"Okay. Okay. Okay." Cat chants to herself, then we hear an intake of breath. "Oh god, I touched something wet. And warm. Tarekh!"

"Kiv, get me over there, now," Tarekh growls into the comm.

"I'm standing two lengths away from you," Kivian says. "You don't have to talk into the comm—"

"Yes, I do. Baby, I am coming for you. We're going to board right now. I swear to you."

"Okay," Cat says in a small voice, and I can hear her shudder through the comm. "Please come get me. Please." She sounds far more delicate and frightened than I've ever heard her. No wonder Tarekh's alarmed. Cat's been claws and fire ever since she boarded the *Fool*. To hear her like this is unnerving.

I flex my hands in my gloves. "I'm ready."

"We're doing this early, then?" Kivian asks.

"No question," Fran says. "You're overruled, babe."

Sentorr is silent. Then, he says, "I can pull the *Fool* closer. Cat, do you have the chip still?"

I hear the sound of someone sucking in deep breaths. "I...yes."

"Kef the chip," Tarekh growls.

"No," Sentorr says coldly. "If you want to get her back quickly, she needs to pry off the ventilation panel like we showed her and crawl through to find the wire connections. From there, she just needs to insert the chip and activate it. That's the easy way to do things. If we do them the hard way, it's going to take that much longer."

"Okay," Cat whispers. I hear her sniffle. "Okay. I can do this."

Two seconds later, a wild-eyed Tarekh appears at the hatch. He's got an enormous blaster in his hands, and the look on his face is stony and determined. His tail flicks madly, and he looks as if he'd tear through the hull of the *Fool* in a second if it meant getting to Cat faster.

I nod at him. "You need to leave that behind."

"Kef you."

"You want to blast a hole in the middle of their ship and space your mate?" Kef, why am I the reasonable one? I'm the hothead. The fists. This is bizarre.

His nostrils flare, and I can practically hear his teeth grind. In my ear, Cat sobs through the comm, and Tarekh's tail flicks back and forth with every aching cry she makes. I get it. She's his mate and she's in danger...or she's not in danger and just being cowardly, but that doesn't sound like Cat. We have to get to her. That's all there is to it. I've known the big medic for years and years, but I've never seen him so agitated. For a moment, it looks like he's going to shoot me with the keffing blaster, but then he slowly lowers it, just a touch.

I move forward. "We're gonna get her, ugly. Just calm down." I ease the blaster from his hands. "You know she's not hurt. She's just panicking."

"Cat never panics," Tarekh growls, but he lets me take the gun. "Never."

"I know. Which is why we're getting her sooner." I move to one of the arms lockers and tuck the plas-rifle safely away, then palm the lock to seal it once more.

"Promise me," Tarekh says in a low voice. When I glance over, he continues. "Promise me that if she's dead, you'll put an end to me, too. I won't live knowing that I failed her."

I stare at him. We've been through a lot, he and I, and Tarekh's always been light-hearted and easy-going. This isn't him. But I've never been mated. I don't understand what it's like. This sits wrong with me.

But I also know what it's like to want to die. So I nod.

2

ALYVOS

*I*t takes endless moments for the *Bringer of Many Joys* to ping back that her shields are disabled and the override to board her chimes onto Sentorr's panel. "Got it," he says in the flat, emotionless voice he always uses when we're on a mission. Sometimes I think he must explode privately in his quarters to let all the tension out...or maybe he's just bottling it all inside.

Kivian joins us shortly, puts away his blasters, and then claps a hand on agitated Tarekh's back. He understands what the male's going through.

Everyone holds their breath as the *Fool* glides alongside the *Bringer* and the docking clamps extend. There's a hiss as the transfer portal extends, locking to the other ship. Then we're attached, and Tarekh charges through the airlock the moment it opens.

I'm right behind him, but with a different kind of enthusiasm. He can get his mate. I get to knock heads.

There's a sweetish stink the moment we get inside the szzt ship that even the filters can't quite take care of. The air's warm and musty, a sign that the ship's seen better days and the recyclers are going to give. If I was a passenger, I'd be terrified of being stranded somewhere in deep space on this hunk of shit, but szzt like to run an old girl into the ground. This is probably normal for them. The passageways are cramped, and the moment we get on the ship, Tarekh heads to the right, looking for the cargo bay and Cat's bio-signal.

I go left, heading for the bridge. I'm eager for a fight. Not just for the fact that they tried to "win" Cat from Kivian, or that they've scared her to death, but for the sheer joy of pounding my fists into something until it's pulped.

"Traitors! Thieves!" a voice growls down the hallway, and then the door to the bridge slides shut, locking me out.

Found 'em.

With a wild grin, I move to the locking panel for the bridge and smash my gloved fist into the delicate network of transmitters, connectors, wires and chips. Like on most older ships, it's not protected, and so I'm able to rip out a handful of cords and the panel goes completely black, the power winking out.

I put my fingers against the edge of the door and slowly force it open, just a hair. Just enough to see the two szzt unfurl shock-sticks. Those are used on slaves, but I understand the thought process there—they can't use blasters, and they need a weapon.

Lucky for me, mesakkah aren't all that affected by shock-sticks.

I shove the door back with a mighty heave and plow into the bridge. I don't know if Kivian's behind me. I don't know if they hit me with the shock-sticks. All I know is that the blood is pounding in my ears and roaring through my body, and my fists fly as I attack my opponents. I want them to pay. I want them to hurt. I want them to regret the choices they've made.

I unload on them, my fists connecting with tough, pebbled orange skin. I slam into them with all the force of my body, blows coming fast and hard. My knuckles hurt as my fists connect, but I ignore it, just like I ignore all the various aches and pains that race through my system as I attack. Old war wounds that twinge, the bad knee that never healed quite like it should have after Thresh II—none of that matters. All that matters is the feeling of defeating the enemy.

Making them hurt.

Making them pay.

At some point, I realize that I'm the only one standing on the bridge. The fury recedes from my mind and I'm panting, staring at the blood-spattered panels around me. They blink with star charts and flight paths, noting the original choice of locations and the hastily changed directions recently programmed in. At my feet, the pair of szzt are collapsed, their bodies bloody and broken.

Still breathing, though. Tough bastards.

I nudge one aside with my boot, wondering if I should get Kivian. If I should finish them off. They're battered and unconscious and they present no harm to us. There's no sign of Kiv or Tarekh, though, and I catch my breath, waiting for the bloodlust inside me to subside. For that yawning, empty ache in my gut to be filled, even temporarily, by the satisfaction of hurting my enemies.

I just feel emptier than ever, though.

Frustrated, I put my gloves together and crack my knuckles. Pain shoots up my hands—a good feeling—and I storm out of the bridge.

Maybe there'll be something—or someone—else to fight in the cargo bay, because I'm not tired. I haven't had enough.

There'll never be enough, my mind whispers, but I ignore it. Have for years and years.

I stalk off the bridge and down the dark, shadowed hallways. No one else comes out to confront me, and I force open door after door to make sure that we're not missing anyone. The ship seems to be empty, so I'm guessing the szzt I just pounded into the floor are the only occupants.

Disappointing. I'm still itching for a fight.

I flick a button on my wrist-comm, looking for the bio-signals of the others. They're still clustered in what must be the cargo bay. I head in that direction, kicking aside debris and slamming a fist into the wall as I go.

The smell of the cargo bay hits me before I get there.

Immediately, I recognize the sickly-sweet stench. I didn't pick it up before, but I do now. Anyone that survived the Threshian war knows what the stink of the dead smells like. It's this cloying, horrific scent that worms into your senses and won't leave. It's greasy and disturbing and brings up a ton of bad memories for me. The very air feels like it's filled with rot and sludge.

The cargo bay stink is like a wall when I turn down the corridor toward it. At the far end of the hall, I see Kivian, a grim look on his face. He shakes his head and slowly steps away. "You don't want to see that, Alyvos."

He knows that I struggle with old war memories. But now that

I've smelled it, I can't not see it. I have to know, if nothing else to put my mind at ease. Sometimes my imagination's worse than anything I can ever see.

I step inside, though, and I realize that no, it's as bad as I thought it was. Off to one side, Cat's collapsed in Tarekh's arms, shuddering as he strokes her hair. He barely glances at me as I enter, his attention fixed on his mate. I'm surprised he hasn't taken her back to the ship yet, but maybe they were waiting for me. Maybe Cat can't walk yet because she's too affected. Or maybe it's only been moments since we boarded. Time blurs when I'm in one of my rages.

This place looks like a slaughterhouse in one of the old vids. The smell of dead things is everywhere, the air hot and stagnant. Old, dark splatters cover the walls, and the floor is filthy with a crust that I'm sure has nothing to do with dirt. Cages are stacked into one shadowy corner of the room, but nothing's moving inside them. I doubt anything's alive.

I doubt anything's been alive in here for a long, long time.

My nostrils flare as I walk in, assessing the place. It makes old memories flare. Bad ones. I shove them back, because everyone was affected by the war. Everyone suffered. I'm not special in that aspect. Special because I can't move on from it, maybe. I stare at the room. At first glance, it just looks messy. No, *trashy*, as if there's piles of rotten garbage that the szzt never threw away or recycled. They just shoved it into this room and let it rot. But those cages make my hackles stand up, and when I step forward and see a pair of curved bones that can only be ribs jutting out from one of the "trash" piles, I realize that it's not garbage.

It's people.

Or it was people.

I rub my jaw, saying nothing. We knew these weren't good guys. We knew that, and that was why we felt no compunction about stealing from them. But this...this is bad. This is beyond what anyone could have imagined.

"Collars," Cat sobs against Tarekh's chest. "They're everywhere. I tripped over one when they shoved me in here and fell into all that mess." She gags, swiping her hands against her clothing. "I'll never feel clean again."

She's not wrong. It's going to take her a long time to get past this. I know that feeling.

I feel curiously detached as I pluck a stray cord off of one old cage. It's not cord, but a lead rope for a slave collar, one I've seen humans wear plenty of times. One that Cat's wearing right now. It's covered in dried blood. There's something rotten at the bottom of the cage and I realize I'm staring at an old corpse of a human.

All of these are old human corpses. Pieces of them anyhow. Mutilated, discarded pieces of people that met a bad, bad ending. I've seen vids of racer kennels on the black market that were raided by authorities and found to be cruelly mistreating their animals. This reminds me of them, except that when I look into one collapsed, rusted cage haphazardly stacked atop another, I don't see the snout of a racer. I see a desiccated five-fingered hand that once belonged to a delicate human much like Cat and Fran. This human died in her cage. So did the one below her. If I had to guess, I'd say every one of these trashed, filthy cages once held an unfortunate human.

No wonder Cat freaked out.

Anger burns in my gut. I drop the lead chain and am silent as I look to Kivian. "Two of the bastards on the bridge. Still alive. Mostly."

He crosses his arms and nods slowly, and I can tell this is a lot for him to swallow. Kiv didn't see the same action I did in the war. This'll be new to him. "What happened here?"

I glance around at the stacked, scattered cages, the bits of material—and other bits—scattered in the dark depths of the cargo bay. "They like to break their toys, it seems."

Cat gags. "I can't believe I volunteered for this."

"Never again," Tarekh grinds out, his tail tightly wrapped around his mate, as if that can somehow make it better. "Never leaving the ship again."

"Oh, kef off with that." She lightly slaps at his chest and sniffs. "It couldn't be helped."

"Yes, it could have," the big male growls. He's not going to let Cat out of his sight for a while, I suspect. He helps her to her feet, then picks her up in his arms. She gives a little protest, but when his tail tightens around her waist, she sighs and puts her arms around his neck and clings to him, giving in and seeking comfort.

I don't watch as they go. I don't need to, because I know Tarekh's going to murmur soft words of comfort to Cat and hold her close until her terror subsides. It's what I'd do.

Kivian waits behind. When Tarekh and Cat are gone, he glances at me. "I haven't said anything to Fran. I turned off comms the moment we realized Cat was fine. So the crew is still alive?"

"Not for much longer." I'm about to go back to the bridge and take care of things, because those bastards are not breathing more oxygen if I can help it.

He nods. "I'll help. We can get the guns later. For now, we should check for survivors, too."

I give him an incredulous look. "Survivors? Look around you, Kiv.

These guys weren't interested in survivors. They were interested in making a keffing mess. They were interested in pulling things apart just to watch them scream. You think they'd leave anything alive?"

Kivian's normally laughing face is somber. "I don't think they would, no. But then I think of my Fran, and I know I can't leave here without checking first."

"We should set this entire keffing ship on fire and launch it into the nearest asteroid, that's what we should do." I kick one of the discarded, bloody collars across the floor. It doesn't go far. It lands in a puddle and stops, and for some reason, that just makes me angrier. "Execution is too quick for those bastards. They need to hurt and they need it to last for a long keffing time. New plan. We hurt them for a while." I put my hands together and crack my knuckles.

"We can do that," Kivian agrees, arms crossed. He still doesn't look sold on my idea. "Or we can get the guns, check for survivors, and make this quick. You forget that we're still in Rakhar IV's airspace. You think someone won't notice the distress signal they sent? Because you know they sent one. Truth is, as much as I'd love to torture those szzt and make them suffer, if we want to protect ourselves and our crew, we need to leave. Fast."

"Kef that. Don't you want to avenge your mate's people?" I gesture at the cages. "Aren't you angry?" Because I'm furious and I don't even have a human mate.

"Of course I'm angry." Kivian narrows his eyes at me. "But I'm also the captain. I need to think about the safety of all of the crew, and the longer we stay here, the more likely it is that we'll get caught. So we do a cursory check and then we get the kef out of here—"

I snarl, slamming my hand into a cage. It rattles and several others fall over. "Kef that. They deserve to pay. They deserve to hurt like they were going to hurt Cat. You know what Fran would say if she knew you were going to turn tail?" I ignore the fact that Kivian's look gets deadly and that he takes a step toward me. "She'd tell you to 'go fuck yourself' in that human language and—"

Kivian raises a fist, even as I speak, and I'm practically gleeful because I want him to be as angry as I am. I want him to rage with a burning misery in his gut like the one I can't ever get rid of. I want—

"Hello?"

The voice is whisper soft, so fragile I barely hear it.

I pause. My imagination, perhaps—

Kivian's hand slams into my jaw, knocking me backward. I stagger against a couple of cages, the stack breaking my fall. I grin at him as I straighten, because I probably deserved that.

"Shut your keffing mouth," Kivian says, dropping his hand.

"Hello?" The soft voice calls out again. It's somewhere in the dark depths of this room. This time, I know it's not my imagination. Kiv and I stare at each other for a moment. I turn on the emergency light on my wrist-comm and shine it into the gloom.

Nothing but filth meets my gaze. "Who's there?" I call out in the human language.

"Me...I...I'm human." The voice is small and timid, almost as if afraid to speak up. "Please...you speak English?"

"Yes," I call out, shining my light into each cage. I run across a fresher corpse and bite back a groan of disgust, continuing to flick my light as I move deeper into the cargo bay. Kef, how many cages of humans did these things keep? "Where are you?"

"I don't know." The voice is surprisingly calm. I'm a little shocked by that, given how frantic Cat was. I can also tell that the voice is female, too. The timbre's a little different than Fran's husky voice or Cat's sharper one. This one's softer, gentler, and has a lilt to certain words. "Please don't leave me." Her voice turns desperate. "I'll behave."

"We're not leaving you," Kivian says, charging past me and shining his light down what looks like a cramped passageway lined with more cages. "How many of you are there?"

"I think I'm the only one left," the voice calls, and there's a tremble in it. "I promise I'll behave."

Such a keffing odd thing to say. I flick my light through cage after cage, looking for the owner.

"Give us a hint of where you're at," Kivian calls again. "We don't have much time to waste."

"I don't know," the woman says again. "I'm sorry."

But the voice is closer, and I continue forward, checking every cage with my beam. My stomach turns at some of the things I see, but that isn't important right now. What's important is finding this female. She sounds so very calm I'm not entirely convinced it isn't a trap.

A moment later, I catch sight of a female's bare foot, though. I race forward, shining the beam into the cage. She's sitting, facing the wall, with her legs tucked underneath her. Filthy, dark hair cascades down her back and she's clearly starving and dirty. The clothes she has on are mere scraps.

She doesn't turn when I shine the beam of my light, though. "What's your name?" I ask.

"Iris," she says in that same calm voice. "Iris Mayweather."

Kivian comes racing over even as I squat near the cage. I work the latch, but it's rusted shut, and judging from the filth lining her cage, she's been stuck in here for some time. There's a cage above her, and one below, and it looks like the one below has been functioning as a toilet for quite some time. The stink is terrible, but I can't blame Iris. It's not like she had a choice. I'm curious to see her face, though.

"I'll be very obedient," Iris tells us again in that placid voice. "Whatever you want, I'll do it."

"Turn around," I say.

She does, and Kivian shines his light on her features. The first thing I notice is that she's lovely. Dainty despite the filth covering her and the shadows on her face. I can't see what color her eyes are as the shadows hide them. Her features are small and regular, her skin slightly duskier than Fran's. She has dark brows and a round face, and the prominent teats I've learned is a normal thing with humans.

Iris lifts her chin, and both Kivian and I suck in a breath at the same time. Her eyes aren't hidden by shadows. They're gone, nothing but dark, angry scars remaining in their place.

"I'll be very obedient," she says again. "Please."

3

IRIS

I can't let these new strangers know how the sound of their arrival is so utterly terrifying and yet hopeful all at once.

I don't think they're my captors. They smell different. Cleaner, less musky. They haven't laughed at the sight of me sitting in my own filth in my cage. No one's thrown a protein bar at my head just to laugh and see how I react. To demand I thank them because my hard-won obedience is more entertaining than watching me starve.

For the first time in a month, I allow myself to feel hope.

But it's been a very hard month and I can't forget the lessons I've learned. So I sit calmly—even though my heart is fluttering so hard I'm surprised they haven't heard it—and wait. This might be another trick. This might be my captors toying with me, trying to goad me into fighting back again because then they get to maim me again.

As if they needed an excuse. My fingers itch, especially the tip of my pinky that's no longer there. My missing toe, too. The carvings in my leg that are probably someone's initials, or the alien equivalent of "Dave Wuz Here." Not my eyes, though. My eyes never hurt.

Probably because they're gone.

Since that awful day that they were taken from me, I've relied on my other senses a lot more. I can sense a change in the air when one of the aliens kneels down in front of my cage. He's standing close enough that I can just catch a whiff of his breath. It's oddly pleasant...but then again, what wouldn't be compared to the stink of this room?

So I sit and wait. Wait for instructions, or beatings, or something. I've learned the hard way that disobedience only costs you things. I was wild and rebellious once—no longer. Never again. I don't want to lose anything else.

I was quiet when the others with the strange babbling alien language came into the room. When the female started screaming and crying, and when others arrived a short time later. I was terrified, but I've learned through weeks of hell that I can't show my responses. So I sit as quiet and motionless as I can with my fists on my thighs, determined not to make a sound. Not to be disobedient.

Until I heard one speak English. He said "fuck." I know he did.

And so I disobeyed for the first time in weeks, though it might cost me my tongue or my nose or my life. I just...I have to know who's here.

"Your eyes," one of the men murmurs in English, and the sound of my native language—hell, just being able to understand someone—is so welcome that I'd cry if I had tear ducts left.

"They're gone."

"They're gone? That's all you have to say about it?" The one man sounds incredulous, and I catch myself fascinated by the way his tongue caresses the words. He says them strangely, as if English— or anything human—isn't his first language, and it probably isn't. I wonder if he's alien, too. "Just as calm as anything? They're gone? They're your eyes."

I want to pour my heart out. I want to say I know they're gone. I wasn't a good slave and so they punished me because I fought back. And the more I fought back, the harder they hit. They took my finger and my toe and when I still wouldn't stop fighting, they took my eyes. And that did it for me. I haven't fought since. Now I'm the only one alive because I'm obedient. The others are dead. All dead. And I'm stuck here in this cage and have been for a month and I want nothing more than my freedom and the cool breeze of Earth on my face. Please help me because I can't take much more.

But I've learned I can take much more. I'll survive if I have to. So I don't say any of that. I don't know if this is a trap, a test to see how obedient I truly am. So all I say is, "I was disobedient once. I've learned my lesson."

The man exhales deeply, a noise of dismay in his throat.

"Let's get her back to the ship," the other voice says. "Fran's going to kill me if we take much longer. You're coming with us, sweetheart. We're going to take care of you. No one's going to ever hurt you again."

"Okay," I say, since they seem to want a response. My heart thuds with excited hope once more. Is it true? Is it possible?

The men discuss something in low voices, and the fact that they switched languages makes me nervous. Here it comes, then. This isn't the rescue I've been hoping for. It just means I can't trust once more. So I put on my calm demeanor once more and I wait.

"You do that," the one nearest my cage—his voice is closest—says to his friend. "I'll get her out of here and back to the ship."

"Fine. I'll be back after I get the, uh, stuff."

There's the sound of footsteps and I realize someone's leaving. I bite my lip because I want to scream at them to please take me, but I fight it back. I swallow hard and wait. Endless, endless waiting. That's all my life seems to be anymore.

Metal creaks, and I feel my cage shudder. "How the kef do you open this thing?"

My heart beats fast again. "I don't know. No one lets me out."

The man growls low in his throat. "You're never sitting in a cage again if I have anything to do with it. Tell me your name. I forgot it."

"Iris," I whisper. And then the cage creaks and groans, the air shifting.

I can't see it, but I sense that the door is open. A wave of longing rushes through me, but I'm too scared to reach for it.

"Give me your hand," the man says. I don't hesitate, because obedience has been beaten into me. I put my hand out and warm fingers brush against mine.

A shiver runs through me when I realize how big the stranger's hand is. His skin feels different, too. I remember from the few times the others—with the orange, pebbly skin—touched me. Their skin tore at mine and hurt. This man feels luscious, like suede. Pettable. He's not like them. "I...who are you? What are you? Where are the others? The ones that took me?"

"Dead," the man says flatly. "Or at least they will be very soon, if I have anything to say about it. My name's Alyvos. I'm a friend." His tone softens as if he realizes that he's scaring me. "I'm a pirate, but I don't hurt humans. You're safe, I promise."

Promises are easily broken, but I nod, because he seems to want an answer. I'm hopeful, but I won't breathe with relief until I'm gone from this place. I memorize his name with the tongue-twist in the middle and repeat it as best I can. "Alvos."

"Close enough." There's a hint of amusement in his voice. "We'll save the language lessons for later. Can you stand?"

Stand? When he tugs on my hand again, I realize he wants me to get out of the cage. Joy rushes through me and I surge forward before he can change his mind. It's been weeks since I've stretched my legs, though, and they cramp up immediately, sending me lurching forward into open air.

Strong arms move around my waist and I'm hauled against a large body a moment later. He's warm and smells so good and clean that I whimper.

"I've got you, Iris," Alvos whispers, and his breath stirs against my skin. "I won't let you fall."

I'm filthy and I feel unclean and weak, but I also feel...safe. I want to see his face, and the ache of that realization hits me. I'm never going to be able to look at him. Ever. I'm going to be lost in the darkness forever.

No, I can't think like that. I'm a survivor. If I'm going to be blind for the rest of my life, so be it. I'll just use my other senses even more. Like touch and smell. Right now, both of those senses are going haywire thanks to the man holding me against his chest. I press my fingertips against his chest and feel the fabric of a shirt as well as something hard underneath. Armor?

"Can you stand?" Alvos asks me.

"It's been a while, but I can try." I attempt to straighten my legs, but it's painfully obvious that they won't support me. I can't straighten them and they feel weak as noodles. "Just give me a moment."

"Exactly how long is a while?" His voice is an angry growl in my ear and then he swings me into his arms, princess style. "I'm taking you to med-bay."

"Okay," I say timidly. I want to ask where med-bay is or what's going to happen there, but I've noticed that aliens have volatile tempers, so I keep my mouth shut and do my best to look obedient.

Obedient keeps me alive. Even if I want to scream with joy at being out of the cage, or run away and hide so no one can ever find me again, I'll clasp my hands in my lap and do my best to be calm and placid, like a good little slave. Emotions are too dangerous, and I can't afford to look like anything except the perfect pet.

4

ALYVOS

*a*s I carry my light, fragile burden onto the *Fool*, I notice things about Iris.

I notice she's a little too thin compared to Fran or Cat, because I can see her ribs through the tatters of her clothing, and her collarbones are so prominent they look painful. I notice she's covered in caked filth and her hair is matted and should probably be cut from her scalp it's so badly snarled. I notice the deep scars where her eyes once were have been cauterized, and in a rather haphazard fashion. Given that every ship is equipped with medical supplies and surgical machinery, it's clear that this was just another form of torture by her captors. I notice she sits with perfect, utter stillness, expression bland, her hands clasped against her waist as if this is an everyday pleasant sort of jaunt instead of a rescue.

I notice she has the cutest, tiniest little nose and a dusky-colored mouth that I can't stop staring at. I know I shouldn't, because she's been badly used, but I'm already feeling incredibly possessive towards her.

And angry. I'm so keffing angry right now. Not at her—but at the szzt that held her, and the conditions she's been kept in for so long. I'm angry that she's been hurt and tortured and she's covered in her own filth and yet...she has the mildest demeanor ever, as if none of this bothers her in the slightest.

I'm angry that she's not angry.

But maybe she's in shock. That, I could understand. The hysterics will come later, when she's safe.

Carefully, I take her through the narrow halls of the szzt junker. I move slowly because I don't want to jostle her trembling form, or knock her feet against a wall that she can't see. She deserves so much better than she's been given, and I vow she'll never have reason to fear me. Once I know that she's safe in med-bay, I'm going to return to this keffing ship and finish the job that I should have done before. I'm going to make sure those aliens never harm another human for as long as I live.

Just the thought fills me with an almost unholy anticipation. Soon.

I take her through the docking tunnel connecting the ships, and the moment the air changes, I can feel her stiffen. Her head lifts a little and she looks less relaxed, a bit warier. "I'm taking you to our ship. You're safe. It's called *The Lovesick Fool* because a nice, silly name doesn't make people think of pirates."

She nods, and I wish she'd say more, but she doesn't. It's disappointing. I want to know what's going on in that head of hers, what she's thinking. I'm hungry to hear her thoughts in a way that I've never been with another female before.

Something deep inside me instinctually recognizes her as mine. I've heard other mesakkah talk about it. How when they meet their female, they just know in their gut that she's the one. That the connection is lightning fast and soul-wrenchingly deep. Always thought that was garbage until now.

Now, I think I'd dismember the next person that tries to lay hands on her.

It's not romantic. Not yet. She's too fragile, too wounded. But that's all right. I can wait, now that I've got something to live for. I've always had something to fight for, but this is different.

Everything's different.

"Iris," I murmur, because I want to feel her name on my tongue, and I want to see how she responds to it. "You're going to stay on my ship for a while. Well, it's not my ship. I'm not the captain. I'm the muscle. But I'll make sure nobody messes with you. The rest of the crew are good guys. They're mated, too. They have females, so you don't have to worry about them. Well, except for Sentorr, but he wouldn't touch you. I don't think he's ever looked in a female's direction twice. When he falls for a female, it's going to hit him completely by surprise, I think." Kef me, I'm babbling like an idiot.

She just sits in my arms so calmly, her head slightly cocked to indicate she's listening to me.

I grit my teeth at that serene silence. "You can say something, you know."

Iris licks her lips, as if trying to think of what to say. I'm fascinated by that small flash of pink tongue until she speaks up. "Thank you, Alvos." Then I'm fascinated by the gentle, rolling sound of her voice.

"You don't have to thank me for saving you." When she's silent again, I bite back a sigh of frustration. "I'd like for you to speak up, please, Iris. I don't want you to be afraid to talk around me."

She hesitates, then nods. "All right. I'll try to speak. I'm sorry."

I growl low. "Or apologize. Don't keffing do that either."

Her brow wrinkles and she turns her head in my direction. "Kef-fing?"

I can feel my ears get hot. "Not a human word. Sorry about that. It's, uh, cursing."

"I see."

She's still so bland. I know there has to be fire inside her. She went through hell and back. I just need to be patient and figure out how to coax it out.

I step into the *Fool* and immediately, the air quality improves. I take a deep lungful with appreciation and continue on towards med-bay with my burden tucked in my arms. "We're going to meet Tarekh in med-bay," I tell her as I continue on. "He's going to look at your wounds and make sure everything's all right. We'll get you patched up."

"Thank you."

"You'll be in good hands with him."

I can feel the tension slide over her and she bites down on that dusky pink lip of hers. She swallows, and I'm fascinated by even the tiniest of movements she makes. When was the last time I noticed how anyone swallowed? Kef me, I've got it bad.

"You're leaving me?"

Her voice is utterly calm, but I can feel the tremor that moves through her.

I'm torn. I want to hurt those szzt again, so badly I can taste it. More than that, I want them to know why I've come back to give them another round of pain. I want to see the spark of life die from their eyes. But Iris is holding herself tense now. Even if she doesn't say it, she wants me to stay at her side. Because I'm already feeling possessive and protective of her, I can't help but change my plans. "I'll stay with you."

She nods, but I can feel some of the tension ease from her.

The door to med-bay opens and Fran comes out, snapping an ammo cartridge into a darkmatter blaster. "Oh, Alyvos. You—" She blanches at the sight of Iris's ruined face and staggers backward. "Oh my god."

I shift my weight, holding Iris tighter against me, as if I could somehow protect her from the look Fran is giving her. It's one of pity and horror, and I recognize that expression. It's one I saw for so many years. People would ask me about the war. I'd tell them where I served, and then that look would come across their face.

I hate that look. I glare at Fran. "This is Iris," I tell her, my tone deadly. "She's staying with us for a while."

Fran regroups, giving herself a little shake. "Of course." She switches to English. "No one told me there was another human coming on board. Are there more?" She glances behind me and lowers her gun to her side but doesn't holster it. "Where's Kiv?"

"Still on the junker, taking care of business."

"Alone? You've got to be kidding me." Her voice goes sharp and she lets out an irritated breath. I can tell that her attention goes from the wounded female in my arms to focus on her mate. She gives her head a little shake and pushes past me. "I'm going after that man. I swear he's going to be the death of me. Nice to meet you, Iris, but I have to go give my mate backup."

I want to point out that we wouldn't have left Kivian alone on board if there was a hint of danger, but it's also probably a good idea for Fran to join him anyhow, just in case. Besides, the captain'll appreciate the sight of his small human mate brandishing a blaster and covering his backside. I watch her go and glance at Iris's face to see her expression. She's gone back to blandness again, her hands clasped tight in front of her.

"We're going into the med-bay now," I tell her. "Tarekh's probably going to be there with his mate, Cat. If she makes you feel uncomfortable, you let me know and I'll make her leave."

Something flickers over Iris's face. Surprise. "You would?"

"I would," I tell her solemnly. "You just say the word."

"Okay," Iris says softly. "Is it...that bad?" One trembling, filthy hand goes to her face and hovers at her cheekbone, as if she's afraid to touch the badly sealed wounds herself.

"It's fine," I say abruptly. Because what can I say? Her eyes were gouged out by males who acted like animals and cruelly cauterized, ruining the chance of regenerative tissue being reattached later on. They deliberately marred her beauty. They wanted to break her. "You're beautiful," I tell her, because I can't not. In my eyes, she is. I see beyond the ugly marks and the harm they've done to her.

Her mouth curves faintly. "Are you blind, too, Alvos?"

My heart skips a beat at that smile. For that, I'd do anything. For her, I'd move asteroids and fly through black holes, unafraid.

I'm hers in that moment. Completely and utterly hers.

~

IF CAT'S startled by Iris's appearance, she doesn't show it. She's snuggled up in a blanket on Tarekh's lap and remains in his chair even after the big male gets up to run medical scans on Iris. Tarekh isn't surprised to see her, which tells me that Kiv probably sent him a private message while I carried her back to warn him that we were incoming. Neither one is chatty like their usual selves. Cat's normally sly and loves to tease Tarekh, and the big male is usually full of laughter and easygoing. Today they're both silent, and I imagine Cat's going to struggle with what she experienced for a while.

It's just a reminder to me that Iris needs time. I'll give her all the time she wants, then. If it makes her feel safer to remain silent and calm, she can do that.

Tarekh examines Iris, and I watch her vitals as intensely as he does, maybe more so. She's malnourished, vitamin deficient, and dehydrated. I'm not surprised, given the conditions we found her in. Her body's fighting off an infection, and the long, ugly wound in her thigh needs stitching. She's missing the tip of one finger, one toe, and another toe has been broken. Her muscles are extremely weak and she'll have to spend time each day in med-bay while the computers run her through a few physical therapy machines, but it doesn't look like there's anything fatal. Tarekh gives that prognosis and I breathe out a sigh of relief, which makes my buddy give me an odd look, his tail twitching.

I don't explain myself. I don't have to. I'm sure he can guess how I'm feeling.

"You need a bit of fixing up, but nothing that a good meal and some nutrient injections won't cure. As for your eyes..." He hesitates.

"I know," Iris says. "They're gone. I can't see anything."

Tarekh raises the scanner, moving it over the scarred tissue and hollow sockets. "Normally this would be where I gave a patient a nice pep talk, but I don't have anything good to say about what they did to you. Even the cauterization..." He trails off. "There's nothing that can be regenerated. I'm sorry."

"Thank you for trying," Iris says in that sweet, simple tone of hers.

I clench my jaw as Tarekh gives me a frustrated look. I hate that she's so complacent about all of this. She should be fighting mad. I could understand that. I could understand fear. Instead she's just...placid.

"I'll give you a salve to reduce the scarring and another one for your thigh. Rub it in twice a day until you're out and I'll add you to the ship's bio-logs so we can monitor you and make sure you're not hiding any other health issues. But you've got no parasites or pathogens, so that's a plus. Love, will you hand me one of those plas-gowns behind you?" He glances over at Cat.

"She can have my blanket," Cat says, and unwraps it from her shoulders, offering it to her mate. "I'm not cold."

I turn back to Iris, frowning. Is she cold? But as Tarekh gently drapes the blanket over Iris's thin shoulders, I realize he's covering her near-nudity. Then I'm mad at myself that I didn't think of such a thing. I should have realized she might be uncomfortable.

"You can sleep here," Tarekh begins.

"No," I interject quickly. The med-bay is a small room and usually cluttered with Tarekh's junk. It's not comfortable and I want her to have a nice bed and pleasant places to sit and relax. I want her to be able to stretch out and get comfortable. "She can have my room. I'll sleep somewhere else."

"All right," Tarekh says easily. Then he switches to our native language. "You know that's how it started between me and Cat, right?"

I scowl at him. Cat just smirks in my direction and gives me a sly wink. "I've got some extra clothes that'll fit you," the human female says. "What did you say your name was again?"

"Iris."

"Like the flower. Pretty." Cat hops to her feet and heads out of med-bay. "I'll be back in a bit."

Tarekh's tail flicks a little slower and he turns away from Iris. He puts away some of his tools and digs out new ones. "Let's go ahead and get that leg wound cleaned and stitched up." He moves to the machine and starts punching something into the interface. As he does, I study her. Her name means "flower"? It suits her and is as lovely as she is.

She turns her face toward my direction, seeking something. "Are you still here, Alvos?"

"I'm here." She gives a little nod and chews on her lip, as if she wants to say something but is afraid. "What is it?" I ask. "Are you in pain?"

Iris swallows hard. "Are you...going to stay?" Her face pales. "You don't have to, of course. I'm sure you're busy. I was just curious..."

"Of course," I tell her, and take a few steps closer. "Do you want to hold my hand while he works on you?"

She immediately sticks her hand out, and I see that it's trembling. Of course she's nervous. I imagine anyone cutting into her after what she's been through is terrifying. I put my hand in hers and give it a squeeze to let her know that I'm here. Iris immediately clasps both hands around mine, and to my surprise, she uses the fingers of her other hand to trace my knuckles. "You only have four fingers," she murmurs. "I thought your hand felt different."

Tarekh looks rather busy across the room, digging through a box of supplies. I rub my thumb over Iris's skin, not caring that she's filthy. "My people have three fingers and a thumb, yes. Same with our feet."

"Your feet have three fingers and a thumb?" That teasing smile curves her mouth again and then immediately disappears once more. "I'm sorry. I shouldn't have said that. I—"

I chuckle, though the sound is forced. I don't like the terror that comes across her face, as if she's just made a grave error by making a joke. I need her to know I'm not upset, though. "My feet are ugly, but not quite that bad."

"No, they're pretty bad," Tarekh adds, returning to her side. He pulls down a pointed-looking attachment from the wall and guides it toward her. "All right, Iris. I'm going to have to open the wound so we can get rid of the infection before it spreads to your bloodstream. I'm going to sterilize the area first, then numb it. Okay?"

"Okay," she breathes, and her hands tighten on mine, though outwardly she's as placid as ever.

I give her a squeeze back to let her know that I'm here.

"You're going to feel something wet across your thigh first," Tarekh says. "Then I'll numb it with a small, painless injection."

I'm pleased that Tarekh's taking the time to explain what he's doing before he touches her. He's a good guy, my friend. I'm buying him a round at the drink bubbler at the next cantina, that's for sure. I rub my thumb over Iris's soft, strange-colored skin again. "If he hurts you, it's okay to get angry at him," I tell her, hoping for a reaction. Laughter. A smile. Something. Anger, even.

But she just remains perfectly still, waiting.

5

IRIS

I don't know if I can trust Alvos, but I desperately need to hold on to someone. I clutch at his strange hand, because it feels comforting and strong, even though I've barely met him. He seems kind enough. I'm aware it might all be an act. That this might be another ploy by my captors to break me in new, fresh ways. To let me think I'm being rescued all so my guard will go down and my reaction will be that much stronger when I'm betrayed again.

I'm aware of this, and still I cling to Alvos, because the thought of being hurt again terrifies me.

I try to remain unmoving, to be calm, but the moment the newcomer, Tarekh, touches my leg, I jump. Memories flash through haunted corners of my mind, of pain and blood and bad things that I'm trying to forget. "Sorry," I yelp out.

"I need you to be still," he says. "This is just the sterilizing pads." Something wet swipes across my leg, brusque and businesslike as he rubs over the wound. Even though it's scabbed over, it hurts when he does that, and I jerk again. He lets out the smallest of sighs at my actions. "You might need to hold her, Alyvos."

I suck in a breath, because the thought terrifies me. Being held down while someone hurts me? It's like my worst nightmares come back to life. I try not to let it show, though, because I've learned that my feelings no longer matter.

The hand I'm holding tenses in mine, as if he can sense my fear. "No," he says, and his tone is firm. "No one's holding her against her will ever again. If Iris doesn't want you to touch her leg, she can say no."

I want to sob with relief at that.

Tarekh sighs heavily this time. "You're being a stubborn fool, Alyvos. Shouldn't you be helping Kivian on the other ship?"

"Iris needs me here," he says simply, and his thumb rubs against my skin. That small touch reassures me. It reminds me that he's promised not to hurt me. Even though it might destroy me to get betrayed again, I believe him. I have to believe in something.

"I'll try to be still," I whisper, and I tighten my grip on Alvos's hand. I know that's not his name. Not all of it anyhow. There's a little twist in the middle of his name that's fascinating and unique. I could probably emulate it reasonably well, but...I haven't. It's a small test to see how he reacts to my mangling of his name, so I know what to expect. Each time I say it wrong to him, I tense, waiting to see if he'll slap me or correct me or his quiet confidence will turn sour.

He hasn't said a thing, though.

"You're fine, Iris," the alien holding my hand tells me. He puts his other hand over our joined ones and now his two hands are warmly clasping mine. It's reassuring, and I only jerk a little when Tarekh drags the abrasive, burning pad over my leg wound again.

I endure the cleaning and then gasp when something hot pierces my leg.

"I need you to be really still for this part," Tarekh says, though he sounds less impatient now. "It'll hurt less that way, I promise."

Well, that's definitely the right thing to say. I do my best to be still even though I'm sweating from terror and bad memories are making me quake. I'm glad in a sick way that I can't see what he's doing because that would be ten times worse. I concentrate instead of Alvos's hands on mine and how they feel. He's got calluses, I notice, and for all that he's only got three fingers and a thumb on each hand, they feel big and warm and comforting. His skin is incredibly soft and I think of suede again. I concentrate on it, wondering if it's just my imagination or if all of him feels like a fuzzy bunny. It's oddly relaxing to picture my rescuer as a masculine-sounding bunny.

I pet his hand, imagining him with floppy ears, a pink, twitching nose, and the warmest, friendliest eyes. I like the thought, and it's comforting enough that I don't realize that Tarekh's done until something cool and wet is smeared over my leg.

"That should seal it for now," the medic says. His hands leave my leg and I realize the pain is gone, too. I relax a little at that. Tarekh continues to speak. "We'll check it again in the morning and I'll put you on a round of human-safe antibiotics. For now, though, you're free to go after I give you a couple of shots."

Free to go. Go where? I'm in outer space, now on a pirate ship if what they're telling me is correct. I'm still at the mercy of the people around me. But I bite back the stab of resentment and nod, keeping my expression calm and bland. "Thank you very much."

There's a long pause, and then Tarekh clears his throat. "I'll, uh, just see what's taking Cat so long with those clothes." There's a hiss of sound that I realize is a door, and then it gets quiet again.

Alvos's hand is still in mine. "Are you all right now? If it hurts, tell me and I'll get Tarekh back in here."

"I'm fine," I tell him, because even if everything hurt, I don't want to be a burden. If these truly are my saviors, the last thing I want to do is become a problem that has to be dumped off on someone else...and I'm already blind. I'm already going to need more help until I get acclimated. I know a lot of people back on Earth get by just fine without their sight, but this is new to me, and until I get used to it, I'm going to struggle.

He grunts, as if he doesn't quite believe me.

Alvos has been the nicest out of the group so far. I wonder if I can ask him questions without him getting upset. Or are bunny-people foul-tempered? He was strong, I remember that from him lifting me and carrying me. But so far he's been patient, even kind. If I ask something and he gets offended, though, I might lose a finger...or worse.

It might be worse not to know, though. "Alvos...are we in here alone?"

"Of course."

I weigh this response and decide that even if he's not telling the truth, it doesn't matter. "What do you plan to do with me?" I ask him.

He considers for a moment, and then his clothing rustles. A shrug, perhaps? "I don't know yet."

At least he's honest, but his answer still fills me with dread. He did say they were pirates, and I know what these aliens all seem to think of humans. That we're little more than playthings for them, things without brains or feelings. The fact that he doesn't know what they plan to do with me means that I might have to earn my keep.

If I have to do it on my back, I will. I just never want to be in a cage again. "I won't fight you if you want to touch me," I offer. "I'll be good."

The alien makes a disgusted sound and his hand slips out of mine. "That's not what I meant."

He sounds angry, and fear makes me tremble. I can't afford to have him upset at me. He's been my champion so far and I need to stay on his good side. "I'm sorry."

Alvos makes another upset sound. "Iris, quit keffing apologizing. I'm not going to hit you."

Hitting me? I'd be lucky if that was the only punishment for an unreasonable slave. I don't know what response he wants, though, so I remain silent.

I hear the sound of steps and the air moves slightly, as if he's pacing back and forth in front of me. "I need you to trust me when I promise that no one's going to hurt you here. No one's going to use you for that, either. You're safe. When I say I don't know what's going to happen with you, it's because I can't make choices for the rest of the crew. We all have a say in who stays on the ship. If it's up to me, you can stay. Worst comes to worst, we'll take you somewhere safe where they'll take care of you."

I remain silent. It sounds nice, but I've learned not to trust anyone or anything. The only thing I can control is the way I present myself. Pleasant. Harmless. Unassuming. So I smile at him as if that's a terrific answer that has solved all of my questions. "Thank you."

He sounds disgruntled at my response, and I worry I didn't sound enthusiastic enough.

6

ALYVOS

*I*ris infuriates me. I've only known her for an afternoon and yet I feel like she's changed my life...which is why it's all the more frustrating that she won't let me in. Since I'm watching her so intently, I can see when she closes off. I can see there are many different answers underneath the bland responses she gives me. But I can't pry yet. She doesn't know me or trust me.

It's frustrating, but I'm not going to give up. I'm never going to give up on her.

She sits on the table with the blanket hanging off her shoulders, and I notice that her hands have gone back to that tight clasp in her lap. It's the same pose she had when I found her in the cage, and it makes me uneasy to see it. In my mind, that's her waiting-to-die pose.

I need to shake her out of it...without touching her of course.

Even though she held on to my hand sweetly while Tarekh worked on her leg, I don't think the trust is there yet for me to grab her, not when she can't see me. So I cross my arms over my chest and lob questions at her. "Are you tired? Hungry? Thirsty? Need to use the bathroom? Shower?"

Her head tilts with interest, her lips parting. "Shower? You have a shower?"

"That's the human word for it, isn't it? A water spray that cleans you?"

"Yes!" Iris fingers one filthy lock of hair. "I...I'd love to get clean. Will it be all right with my leg?"

"Why wouldn't it?" I'm curious.

"Because Tarekh just bandaged it?"

Ah. "You mean the plas he spread over the wound? It'll repel water and remain in place until you peel it off. It's fine. You can shower for as long as you like."

She sucks in a breath. "Really?" Her voice is faint with disbelief.

"Really. The water's filtered and recycled, so it's not like you can waste it."

A slow smile spreads across her cheeks. It's beautiful, which is what makes the cruel red marks on her eyelids so heart-rending. I swallow hard. If Kivian hasn't destroyed those szzt yet, nothing's going to stop me from putting my hands around their repulsive throats.

"Can we go shower now?" Iris asks, her voice shy. "It's been forever since I've been clean."

My cock reacts to her words. Can we go shower. But I know she doesn't mean it like that. She can't. Even if she did, it's not her choice, she's just telling me what she thinks I want to hear. "Of course. It's in my quarters. Come on."

There's the slightest hint of hesitation, but she pins a smile on her face. "Okay."

I'm starting to hate every time she says "okay" because I suspect she'd love to say something else instead. I imagine myself in her shoes, and I suspect she's uneasy at the thought of going to my quarters.

"They'll be your quarters while you're with us," I tell her. "I'll sleep outside the door to make sure you're not bothered. Not that anyone would bother you. I'm just saying if it'll make you feel better." Great, now I'm second-guessing everything that comes out of my mouth. "Come on, I'll take you there."

I brush my fingers over the back of one wrist to let her know where I'm at. She grips my hand tightly, putting both of hers on mine as if I'm the only thing she can trust. It's humbling, and I vow never to break that trust.

I guide her down one of the halls of the *Fool* and notice that no one else is around. Normally the ship seems cramped—especially now that we have two humans and four mesakkah when it's supposed to be a four-crew vessel. But today everyone's vanished. Either Fran's still helping Kivian with the other ship and Tarekh's finding Cat, or everyone's deliberately avoiding Iris to give her space. Either way, I'll take it. As we walk, I notice she leans closer and closer to me, her arm pressed against mine. Her steps are shuffling and weak, though at least she can walk now. It's proof that the shots Tarekh gave her were good for her.

We don't make it halfway down the hall before she needs to stop and take a break, though, and I'm reminded that it's been a while since she's stood, much less walked. I'm a keffing idiot. I scoop her up into my arms, half expecting her to protest. She doesn't, of course. She's utterly silent but clasps her hands tight in her lap, and I know it bothers her.

I give the verbal command for the door to my chambers to open, since I don't have a free hand to use the bio-scanner. It chimes politely and then the door slides back, and I make a mental note that I'll have to give Iris access so she doesn't lock herself out of my room when I'm not there. As if I'm going to leave her side for long. Already I imagine she's going to get sick of me long before I get sick of her.

When we enter my room, the door slides quietly shut behind us and I know Iris can't see anything, so I try to describe it. I'm not good with flowery words, though. The best I've got for her is mentioning the furniture and that some of it is located along the wall. I'm trying, though. I carry her into the water closet—what the humans call a bathroom—and set her down gently.

I'm not sure how familiar she is with our technology, so I take her hand and show her panels, explaining how to turn the water in the sink off and on, how to get soap, and how to make the toilet work. I lead her to the glassed-in box of my shower and show it to her, and my heart aches when a shy smile curves her mouth at the touch of water on her fingertips.

Kef, I love that smile. I'd do anything for it.

"So...that's all there is to it," I tell her brusquely. "You're free to use any of this for as long as you like."

"Thank you," she says, and this time it seems genuine. She immediately begins to peel off her filthy rags, and I turn away. It seems wrong to watch her get naked, even though I know she wouldn't be able to see that I'm watching her.

I'd know, and that makes all the difference in the world.

"I'll just be outside." I get up and head for the door, averting my gaze. I let it slide shut behind me and lean against the wall, closing my eyes. My cock aches. My pulse throbs in my veins and I would give anything to be able to go into that room and touch her.

She's not ready for a male, though. Not after what she's been through. She might never be ready.

This must be how Tarekh felt when Cat was brought on board. Or Kivian when he acquired Fran...except both of those women were independent and strong and talked back if anyone gave them crap. Iris is strong, but in different ways. She's quiet and she won't do anything but smile at you...but she has to be strong to have survived what she did. I can't imagine. Even in my darkest days on Thresh II, I never had to endure what she did.

A whimper catches my attention. I push off the wall, wondering if I'm imagining things. That it's just my brain playing tricks and I'm too attuned to Iris. She whimpers again, and I hesitate. The sound is soft, and maybe it's just that she aches or that the spray is too hot for her aching body. It doesn't mean that she wants me to charge in there and save her—

"Alvos!" she cries out, the sound terrified and frantic. "Alvos, where are you?"

I slam my hand onto the panel and push through the door the moment it glides open. "Iris? Are you all right?" I enter the room and I'm surprised to see her crouching in the corner of the shower, her back pressed to the walls. She's naked, her arms crossed over her teats, and dirt sluices off of her as the water drips over her body. She's quaking with terror, her head lifting the moment I walk in. "What is it?" I ask again.

Her teeth chatter. "I...please don't leave." Iris's voice drops to a mere whisper. "When you were gone, it felt like I was back there...alone and trapped." She sniffs, and I wonder if she's fighting tears. "I know I shouldn't ask—"

"Don't you dare apologize," I tell her, striding forward. Iris stiffens, and I realize that's the wrong thing to say. "You've been through hell," I tell her as I strip my shirt off my back and toss it aside. I kick my boots off and then I join her in the shower, reaching out and brushing a hand over hers. "If it takes you time to get used to a new place, it takes you time. I told you that you're safe with me, and I meant it." I stroke a hand over her wet, snarled hair as she flings herself into my arms.

"I'm sorry," she begins, and when I growl, she bites the words off. "I...thank you."

"I'm starting to hate how very polite you are," I mutter.

A teary laugh escapes her. "You want me to cuss at you?"

"I want you to show emotion. Tell me what you're thinking. Don't just tell me what you think I want to hear. I'm not them. I'd never hurt you like they did."

She nods, burrowing her face against my chest. I notice absently that she's naked, but it doesn't matter. This isn't about sex or mating. This is about her terror and how she turned to me when she was afraid. I'm going to be her protector, I vow. If it means dancing attendance on her every day for the rest of my life, I'll gladly do so. I hate the trembling that makes her small frame shudder. I hate that she's so scared to be left alone...but I get it.

"When I came back from the war," I begin, my voice hoarse with emotion. I've never shared this with anyone, but I feel the need to share with her. To show her that I understand. "I would press my back against every wall. Never walked down an open corridor because it felt too exposed. I always had to have my back to something. And I wore body armor to bed for years because I couldn't fall asleep otherwise. I'd get too worked up, thinking that someone was going to attack me."

Her hands curl against my skin, tracing the edge of one of my chest plates. "You're wearing armor now. Are you still scared?"

"That's not armor. That's me. My people, we have protective plating over vulnerable parts of our body. We're not all softness like humans." I take her hand and guide it up to my shoulder so she can feel the plates there, feel where they connect to my skin. "But I wore the armor for years. Three, I think. Then one day, I didn't break into a cold sweat at the thought of going to sleep. I didn't think someone was going to attack me the moment my guard was down." I stroke her hair again. "I'm telling you this because it's hard and it takes time, but you'll get there."

"I'll be fixed?" she whispers, and I can hear the hope in her voice. "Like you?"

I chuckle and hold her tight, determined to ignore the ticklish sensations her exploring fingers send through my body. "Oh, I'm not fixed. I'm as broken as ever. But you get better at hiding it. And you get better at being broken."

Iris just sighs and leans against me. Her entire body sags and I wonder how long it's been since she truly slept. How long since she's let her guard down. Fierce protectiveness overwhelms me, and I fight the urge to squeeze her against my chest forever. To make sure that nothing hurts her ever again.

Eventually her trembling stops and her body relaxes. She's still silent, but some of the tension is gone from her form and I'm glad. I rub her shoulder. "All right now?"

"Yes. Thank you."

I start to disentangle myself from her wet, nude body. "I should leave you alone so you can shower."

She clings to me, her face upturned. "Stay, Alvos. Please? I won't be scared if I know you're here."

"You want me to watch you bathe?"

Her cheeks flush under the dirt. "You don't have to watch. Just talk to me."

It's an odd request, and perhaps even a sexual one. I won't let it be, though. Not after what she's been through. Not after she's given me her trust. I give her back another pat and help her to her feet, and then remain in the shower spray with her so she can hold on to my arm. Her legs are still shaky and her strength questionable. She weakly rubs the cleansing foam on her body with one hand, clinging to me with the other.

And so she doesn't feel uncomfortable, I stare straight ahead, letting the water hit my face, and I tell her about the *Fool*. About how Kivian is our captain, and that sometimes he's as un-leader-like as they come, especially for a pirate. How he dotes on Fran, who's the practical one in that pairing whereas Kivian's more of a good-time kind of guy. How Sentorr practically lives on the bridge and practically seems mated to the ship and the nav control panels sometimes. How good-natured Tarekh's both mechanic and medic all in one, and that Cat helps him out and plays tricks on him just because she's got a sassy streak a mile wide and Tarekh secretly loves it. How I'm supposed to be the mechanic on the ship, but Tarekh's the one that likes to tinker with things, so I mostly clean guns and make sure our weapons are at the ready. I'm good when it comes to a fight. I've had years of combat training, have excellent aim, and I can pretty much turn anything into a weapon if needed. I tell her that Kivian jokes that if I were dropped onto a wild planet for a month, they'd come back and find me with a defensible fortress and I'll have conquered the locals. He's probably not wrong. I'm not the type that can sit still or be content with merely existing from day to day. There's a restlessness in my belly that makes me push harder and fight for more. Always more. I'm the first one in a fight and the last to leave.

I worry a little that confessing my bloodthirsty attitude is going to frighten her, but I can't hide who I am. I solve my problems with my fists. I fight to release tension. I'm not the easygoing male that Tarekh is. I'm not full of laughter like Kivian. I'm an angry, broken thing inside and I use my fists to cope. I'd never hurt her, but that's something she'll have to learn, because no amount of me promising that she's safe is going to matter in her eyes. She already doesn't trust.

I won't lie to her, though.

7

ALYVOS

*E*ventually the water runs clean and her skin is a lovely, even shade instead of dirty smudges. Her dark hair is a wet fall over her shoulders and she looks better. Even her color is improved, as if just washing up has made her heart lighter. She wipes water from her face and pauses as her fingers slide over her eyes, as if she's forgotten that there's nothing but scars there. The smile on her mouth fades ever so slightly.

"I think I'm done," Iris says in that polite, even voice of hers. "Thank you, Alvos."

"Don't make me growl at you," I tell her. "You're allowed to shower as much as you want on this ship."

Her wet fingers—the tips shriveled from the shower—caress my forearm. "Yes, but thank you for standing here with me and being with me. And talking. And not leaving me alone." She holds me tight. "I don't think I like being alone anymore."

"I understand." And I do. I think I understand that more than anyone. "Come on. Let's get you dried off."

I wrap a plas-towel around her shoulders, and she flinches and then holds herself very still as the fabric adjusts to her body. I explain to her that it's normal, but I can tell she's unsettled. She lightly strokes the material as if she doesn't quite trust it not to move. I lead her out of the water closet and then over to my bed. For once, I'm glad that I'm tidier than Tarekh. My bed is made with the blankets pulled tight. I don't have pillows like humans like to use, and I make a mental note to get one from Fran or Cat.

I guide Iris to the side of the bed and she sits down delicately. "I'll find Cat and see where she is with those clothes."

She clutches my arm. "It's all right. They can wait. Do you have scissors? Or a knife?"

"I do...why?" Is there a human bathing ritual I'm unaware of?

"I need to cut my hair off." She pushes it back from her face with a grimace. "It's just one big knot."

"You don't like it?" I can't resist taking a lock of it between my fingers and rubbing. It's wet and knotted, but the strands are like silk.

"I'll never get it detangled. It's too snarled."

"I'll do it for you."

Her lips part with surprise. "You will?"

In this moment, there is nothing I want more. Tend to her? Take care of her? Make her feel comforted and loved? "Gladly. Wait here and I'll return."

I head to the water closet and grab my comb. It's wide-toothed for mesakkah hair, which has a different texture than human hair. It should still do the trick, though, and when I return to the bed a moment later and touch her shoulder, Iris relaxes and smiles back at me, and I feel as if I've won a prize just for volunteering to take care of her.

She should be pampered all her days, not treated like she was. Just the thought of what she's been through makes the rage burn in my gut. For a moment, I want to throw the comb down on the bed and chase down Kivian and see what happened with the szzt and their ship. See if they were disposed of or if there's still someone for me to destroy. But I'd have to leave Iris's side and it's clear she doesn't want to be left alone. Even that small window in which I left her side to get the comb made her tense and worried. She's relaxed now that I'm back, and I take a handful of her hair and begin to gently work through the snarls.

If I have to choose between Iris and my revenge, I choose Iris. It's a first for me to give up on a chance to fight, but Iris needs me. Kivian knows how I feel about those szzt, and I trust him to take care of things. I relax and focus on Iris's hair, and I don't even mind when the floors of the ship begin to vibrate, signaling that we're accelerating and no longer docked to the junker.

I do my best not to yank on her hair, but she's right—it's snarled to the point that I'm not surprised she wanted to cut it off. As it dries, though, it changes to a rich dark brown and clings to my fingers, soft and pettable. I'm glad she's letting me do this, because I think it's beautiful. She's silent as I work, her hands in her lap. I want her to speak, even if it's just for the pleasure of hearing her thoughts. "I've told you about me. Tell me about you, Iris."

"There's nothing important to tell," she says in that mild voice of hers.

She's wrong, but she's also got that passive tone in her voice that tells me she's going to keep her secrets. That's all right. She just got here. It's early for her to trust, but I hope that someday she'll share more with me. "If you say so."

"How did you learn the human language?" Iris asks, just as the door chimes and announces Cat's presence outside.

"Open," I call out, and the door slides back.

Cat steps inside, and then pauses when she sees Iris perched on the bed in a plas-towel and me combing her wet hair. She raises one of those mobile human eyebrows at me, and I scowl in her direction. I don't care what it looks like. "Sorry to interrupt this scene of domestic bliss, but I brought clothing." She gestures at the bundle in her hands. "Should I come back later?"

"Don't be ridiculous," I half snarl at her. Cat just smirks in my direction, not put off by my bad temper. "I was just helping Iris with her hair. We can finish it later. She probably wants clothing more than a combing, and I need to check in with Kivian." I press the comb into Iris's hand and give it a squeeze. "Can you stay with her until I get back?"

"Of course," Cat says in a cheery voice. "I brought several different things in case you don't like some of what I have. I'm a big fan of choices." She plops herself down on the floor near the bed and starts to spread things out before her. "Take your time, Aly. We're good here."

I'm sure she is, but I worry about Iris. "Will you be good?" I ask with a touch to her shoulder.

"Of course." Her voice is smooth and pleasant. "Thank you."

I grit my teeth at how robotic and monotonous she makes those words sound. So very agreeable. But I don't want to call her out on it in front of Cat. Everyone's got their defense mechanisms. I just give her another pat on the shoulder and head out of the room. I shut the door and pause outside for a moment, just in case Iris starts screaming in fear. Just in case she needs me. When it's quiet, I leave and head for the bridge.

Only Sentorr is there, bent over the nav panels of the *Fool* as if they provide all the answers of the universe.

"Where's Kivian?" I ask.

"He and Fran are unavailable at the moment," Sentorr says, his tone indicating he doesn't approve."

Ah. That means they're mating. I head to my chair in one corner of the bridge—the security station—and sit down, kicking my feet up on my panel and trying to look comfortable and at ease. Instead, I'm wondering about Iris and how she likes Cat. If I should go back because she needs me there, or if I'm just being overbearing.

Probably overbearing.

I glance over at Sentorr, who's watching me with the corners of his hard mouth turned down slightly. I study him. There's not a hair on his head out of place, his horn coverings immaculately polished. He's even wearing a uniform, which is ironic because the *Fool* has no uniforms. If we did, though, I imagine they'd look like the stiff, uncomfortable creation he's wearing, with a million buttons on the front and a high collar to choke the life out of a male. And decorative sleeves, I add mentally. Damned Kivian loves a decorated sleeve. Sentorr's personality is as buttoned up as his clothing, though. He gives me another look of disapproval, gaze flicking from my feet up on the panel to my face.

I rub my jaw, thinking absently of the female I left behind in my quarters. It feels strange to be sitting here on the bridge, pretending to relax when I'm anything but. I feel an overwhelming need to return to her side, and I fight it, because I don't want to come across as too possessive. Not until she's ready to think about me as something other than her rescuer. Like I said before, it might be never.

But if my hellish time during the war taught me anything, it's that perspectives change over time. Old wounds fade even if they don't go away. So I can be patient and play the long game.

I force myself to cross my arms over my chest and study the nav charts pulled up on the screens as if they hold my interest in the slightest. They don't. Sentorr doesn't offer information and when he turns back to his nav charts, I speak up. "The junker?"

He flicks a glance over at me. "Currently having a system malfunction and en route to the nearest sun. No life on board, if that's what you're asking."

"That's what I'm asking," I agree, pleased. Kivian took care of business. Good. It's the ugly side of piracy, but sometimes things get ugly. I don't regret it. I only regret I wasn't the one that got to pull the trigger so Iris could hear from me that they're finished.

Iris. I can't stop thinking about her. Strangely enough, I don't think about her scars or the painful-looking shadows where her eyes should be. I think about that hint of a smile that sometimes curves her lips and how I'd do anything for it. I wonder if it's too soon to go back and check in on her. If that'll seem weird.

"Not you, too." Sentorr's voice is sour.

I look over at my friend. He's tapping away at the nav charts, updating our path and scanning communication bands to ensure we avoid the law. He's always busy with something, Sentorr. Always focused on the *Fool*. It makes me wonder what's going on in his head sometimes. If the male's ever heard of "downtime." Of what he's trying to avoid by burying himself in work. Of course, I don't ask. Never would. "Not me too what?"

His mouth turns down and he jabs one of the panels a little harder than necessary. "She's your mate, isn't she? It's obvious to me that we've acquired yet another human to squeeze into our four-crew ship." The disapproval drips from his tone.

"It's that obvious already?" I don't deny it. The moment I lifted Iris into my arms, I knew she was mine.

"It is. There's something about you that's different. Changed."

Huh. Funny how that shows outwardly. I feel changed, too. Rejuvenated. Like I have a new focus in life that doesn't just involve bloodying my knuckles. "Yeah. She's mine. I didn't think it'd happen so fast but…"

"I hear that's how it happens," Sentorr says, flicking a hand over his screen and pulling up another map, then overlaying it on the current star chart. "Like a bolt of lightning."

He's not wrong. I always thought that was a tall tale myself, but one look at Iris and something in me shifted. The hollow places got filled by the sight of her. I'm not even the slightest bit upset about it. Thought I'd fight it more when the time came, because I'm all jagged edges inside. But something about Iris just feels right. Feels good. Feels like she needs me as much as I need her. She's still got too many secrets, but that's all right. There's time enough for everything to come out. She'll share when she's ready.

Of course, that means everyone on the *Fool* is matched up except for Sentorr. I watch him as he works busily, his tail flicking in time to the movements he makes across screen after screen. Is he lonely? I didn't realize I was until I saw Iris. "Someday it'll happen for you, too, my friend."

He just snorts.

8

IRIS

I feel vulnerable, left alone in Alvos's room with a stranger. I can sense the woman nearby on the floor, humming a little tune to herself as she does something and makes fabric rustle.

"These don't have human sizes, I'm afraid," she says after a moment. "They're mostly utilitarian jumpers, but they're comfy enough. I grabbed a few that are standard fabric and one that's plas. Like the towel you're holding, it'll modify itself to mold to your shape."

Her tone is friendly and pleasant, but there's something about it that's familiar. "You're the one on the ship, aren't you? The one they brought in?" I heard someone screaming in terror. Screaming as she was put into one of the filthy cages that stank of rotting things, and the laughter of the aliens. I remember her whimpers of terror and then the harsh, angry notes she spoke into the air as she demanded that someone come get her.

Through all of that, I never spoke up. I couldn't. Not if it meant that I might get punished again. Maybe I should have tried to comfort her, or let her know I was there, but my tongue was locked in my mouth and terror kept my lips sealed.

I hope she doesn't hate me for it.

"That was me," the woman says. "I'm Catrin, but everyone calls me Cat. And yeah, it was my stupid plan to get myself captured so I could infiltrate their ship like a badass, but it went a little bit awry." Her voice is self-deprecating. "I screamed like a little bitch the entire time, but I also wasn't exactly expecting a slaughter-house." There's a pause and her voice gets tight. "Still makes me want to vomit thinking about it."

I understand that feeling. In a way, I'm glad I couldn't see how bad it got. "I should have spoken up."

"I didn't know you were there. I'd probably have screamed a hell of a lot more if I did. It's all good. Here, I brought you this. It's a ribbon."

A ribbon? I put my hand out, curious. Is this one of those things where they think humans dress a certain way? I've never worn a ribbon in my life. "Thank you."

"It's for your eyes. So you're not self-conscious over the scars." Something slithery and soft drops into my hand and I feel her fingers brush against mine.

I smile faintly. I want to ask if the scars are that bad, but I can guess. It wounds my vanity, because once upon a time, I thought of myself as fairly pretty. Now the only word that comes to mind is "mangled," and it's hard to think about facing all these new people in the crew of the *Fool* with my scars plainly on my face. Each sucked-in breath hurts my feelings even if I try to ignore it. "Good idea. How did you know?"

"I'm a girl, I know these things." She gives a soft chuckle. "And it's not like we have armor like they do. We have to wear our armor on the inside."

I'm surprised to hear her words, putting us together as if we're the same. I think back to the brush of her fingers against mine and realize she's not softly fuzzy like Alvos. "You're human?"

"Well, yeah." Cat clears her throat. "I'm embarrassed to say I should have pointed that out sooner. Yes, I'm human. Fran is, too."

I can barely breathe. There were humans on the last ship, too. "Are you...here against your will?" Oh god. What if I've been lied to? I've let my guard down already. Betrayal would be so very horrifying and disappointing—

Cat snorts. "Against my will? Hell no. They saved me from a situation like yours. Fran, too. We were both kidnapped humans and the crew saved us. I was given the choice to stay and become part of the crew, or I could leave and they'd take me somewhere safe. I decided to stay, because who's going to harass Tarekh if not me?" She chuckles again, and then I hear the rustle of fabric. A moment later, something soft is placed under my hand. "This is one of your basic tunics. It's made a lot like human clothing, but the fasteners are different. I can talk you through it, or I can help you dress, whichever you prefer."

She's so chatty that it takes a moment for it to sink in for me. Cat's here because she's a human they rescued. Fran, too. And they're not the least bit afraid of the pirate crew. They chose to stay.

Wariness wars with hope. This could all be an elaborate lie. Cat could be deceiving me just like Alvos. But so far everyone's been...kind. It makes me feel like the universe isn't without hope after all. That my ordeal might be over. That I might truly be safe.

An ugly, rough sob catches in my throat.

"Do you need a moment?" Cat asks, her voice all sympathy. She reaches out and touches my hand, and I clasp her fingers in mine. Four fingers and a thumb. She's human. She's safe. They're all safe. I'm in a safe place. A good place.

I want to scream with joy and throw up at the same time, I'm so rattled and full of nerves. I hate that the thought of being safe makes me want to vomit, but fear and hunger have done a number on my stomach over the last few months. "I'm okay," I manage to choke out to Cat. "Thank you."

And this time when I thank someone, I really mean it.

CAT HELPS me finish brushing out my hair and we adjust the ribbon over my eyes. It's about two inches thick, and when I ask, she reassures me that my scars are almost completely covered. There's still a hint of a long slash under the corner of one eye that drags down to my cheek, but that's all right. I feel better with the pretty, delicate covering over my scars. Cat tells me that it's a bright, cheery red, and I picture it over my clean hair and feel almost pretty again. Not that being pretty matters, but clean and new clothes and fresh hair? It's good for the soul and I feel better. Like my old self.

I think that girl is gone forever, but it's nice to imagine some semblance of her still exists.

After I'm dressed, Cat and I sit on Alvos's bed for a while. She offers me snacks from the ship's "dispenser" and offers to take me to the mess hall on the ship to get real food. I decline, because I'm not sure I'm ready to interact with people yet. It's hard enough being around strangers I don't entirely trust. I can't imagine sitting around a bunch of them, unable to see them, forced to make conversation and eat alien food. So I nibble on the strange-tasting bars Cat gives me and drink water, and I'm happy. Even though Cat's not thrilled with it, it's still the best meal I've had in forever and ever. I eat every serving she gives me, though I can't bring myself to ask for more. The need to be unassuming and easygoing so they don't dump me somewhere or punish me isn't easy to ignore. Even though I'm still hungry, I smile and act as if nothing's amiss.

The door chimes. "Entry: Alyvos Nos Sturian." There's a swish and then the air changes. I turn my head automatically toward the door, even though I can't see him come in.

"Hey there," Cat says, and I can hear the rustle of her clothing as she stands up and dusts crumbs off her lap. "We were just having a snack. I think I'll leave you two and go find my honey bun. If you want to hang out, Iris, just give me a shout. I'm always around and it's a small ship." With a little chuckle, I hear her feet pad on the floor and she's gone.

The door swishes shut again, and it's utterly silent in the room. For a moment, panic grips me and I worry that Alvos has left me alone. Heat prickles my skin and I start to sweat at the thought of being trapped in this room without knowing how to get out the door. After all, rooms are squares, right? And squares are just like one big cage, and if I'm stuck here, forgotten—

I force myself to draw in a shuddering breath. "H-hello?"

"I'm here." The smooth bass of Alvos's voice comforts me. I can feel myself relaxing, my shoulders easing. I reach out into the air and then hesitate. Maybe he doesn't like being touched or having a girl cling to him all the time. I need to be independent.

I don't want to be, but I also don't want him getting tired of me.

I'm at the mercy of everyone on this ship, no matter how nice they are. So I pin a smile to my face. "Everything seems to fit."

"You look lovely." There's a husky, pleasant note in his voice that makes me shiver.

I reach up and touch the ribbon covering my scars. "I guess this helps hide some of the worst."

He grunts, and I feel a stab of hurt.

9

ALYVOS

I don't know what to say. I want to tell her that the ribbon doesn't matter. That I love her scars because they show how strong she is and what she's survived. That she couldn't be any lovelier to me no matter what she did or wore, because it doesn't change anything for me. But that'll just scare her, so I grunt.

And her face falls with disappointment. Damn it. I keffed that up. "How are you feeling?"

Her lips part, and then she breaks into a jaw-cracking yawn. A second later, she gives a little grimace of embarrassment that's adorable to see. "I guess I'm tired. I'm sorry. What time is it?"

"Early afternoon."

She bites her lip. "I think my schedule's messed up. Or maybe because it's always dark..." She lets her words trail off and touches the edge of the ribbon.

"You can sleep—"

"Oh no, that's all right." She clasps her hands in her lap and gives me a bright smile. "I'll go to sleep when everyone else does."

"There's no need to wait. No one's going to bother you. I'll show you how to work the basic controls here in the room and get you set up with an identification so you can come and go as you please."

She hesitates. Then, "Thank you."

I grit my teeth as she thanks me again. So much thanking, so much hiding her thoughts. It makes me crazy. I want her to yell at me. I want her to demand more. To tell me that she's hungry or thirsty or that I shouldn't push her to bed because she can do what she wants. But she just smiles and clasps her hands and looks so exhausted that it's pitiful. Her shoulders are slumped and her posture is that of a wilting flower. It's been a long, hard day for her—hell, a long, hard month—and I'm betting that she's emotionally spent, if not physically. Somehow I think if I told her she needed to stay awake until midnight, she'd simply clasp her hands in her lap and sit there with a smile on her face, determined to do just that because she'd want to please me.

I can't wait for the day she realizes that the way she can please me best is to tell me to kef off.

Today's not that day, though. I move forward and take her hand in mine and she jumps a little, startled at the touch. Damn it. "That's my fault," I tell her. "I should have told you I was moving closer."

"Oh, I knew you were moving toward me." Iris tilts her head up at the sound of my voice. "I was just...distracted." Her cheeks are flushed slightly.

"Distracted by what?"

"Nothing important," she says swiftly. "I can sleep on the floor, you know. It won't be a bother. Or anywhere there's a quiet out-of-the-way spot. I don't want to be a burd—"

I growl before she can finish that statement. "If you tell me you're a burden, so help me, I'm going to lose my mind."

Her becoming flush disappears and her face bleaches of color. She leans back, and terror is clear in her body. Kef. I've said the wrong thing again. Her entire body trembles and she holds herself very still. "I'm sorry—"

"Iris," I state calmly. I want to cup her face in my hands, but that'll probably terrify her, so I simply squeeze her hand. "Stop it. Calm down. I'm not going to hurt you if you disagree with me. All right?"

"All right."

I make a frustrated noise. "Are you just telling me that because it's what I want to hear?"

"Yes?"

I can't help but huff a laugh at that.

"I just...this is all very new for me," she whispers. "It's hard for me to remember that I'm not back in the cage. That everything can't change at a moment's notice...again."

"I understand. I just hate seeing you so afraid."

"Then don't look," she retorts, and then goes pale again. "I'm sorry—"

"Don't you dare apologize for that. I loved it." I rub my thumb over the back of her hand. "Now, you're sleeping in my room tonight and I don't want you to tell me that the floor is fine or any other random corner you pick out. You've been through a rough time in the last while. You're barely holding together. You're going to sleep in my bed tonight and that's all there is to it."

Iris looks as if she wants to protest, but she eventually nods. "I'm...a little scared to go to sleep." She licks her lips and her breathing speeds up. "If you leave, I just worry I'm going to wake up and think I'm back there in the cage. I can't stand the thought of that." She caresses my hand and then holds it to her breast-bone. "Will you stay and sleep with me tonight so I'm not scared? It doesn't have to be sexual. I just want the company." She pauses for a moment. "Unless you want it to—"

"Stop," I tell her before she tries to give me something she shouldn't. "Your body is yours. I'll sleep in the room if you want company tonight. It doesn't have to be in the bed. I can sleep on the floor."

"Thank you," she says in a small voice and squeezes my hand. "It's stupid, I know—"

"It's not stupid. You're talking to an ex-soldier that wore body armor for three years straight." Her little smile is heartbreaking, and I want to squeeze her against my chest again. I shouldn't, though. I'm already touching her far too much. "If you're tired, lie down. I'll set you up in the systems in the morning." I can send a note to the others via my wrist-comm that I'm going to be spending time tonight with Iris until she's comfortable. The noble part of me thinks I should sneak out and leave after she's asleep, but if she wakes up, I don't want her to think she's alone.

So I'll stay.

I set the room lights to dim and then change the settings to sleep mode. Soft noise pipes into the room, a peaceful, numbing sort of sound blanket that helps me relax.

She smiles to hear it. "Is that the ocean?"

"Yeah. I can't sleep when it's too quiet. Does it bother you?"

"Not at all. I like it. Makes me think of home. Maybe if I hear that I won't wake up and think I'm in a cage." She lies back on the blankets, her body small and delicate in my large bed.

"You want a pillow? The other humans use them, but I don't have any."

"I'm fine."

I sigh heavily, because even if she wanted one, she wouldn't say anything. I'm learning that about her. "What if I folded up a blanket and you used it as a pillow?"

"If you like."

I decide to do it anyhow, and get my softest blanket from storage. I fold it into a neat square and then move to the side of the bed and set it down next to her cheek. "Here it is."

She sits up and tucks it under her head. "Thank you, Alvos."

I think about the way she mispronounces my name. The other humans don't have trouble with it. Perhaps her tongue works differently than theirs. Humans have great variations in their appearances, so it would stand to reason that they might have different tongues as well. Either way, I don't mind it. I kind of like it. Mine is the only name I've heard her speak so far, and I hope mine is the only one she makes unique. Perhaps that's selfish of me. "Of course. Comfortable?"

"Yes."

"Would you tell me if you weren't?"

"No?" Her voice is small.

I snort and settle in on the floor. It's not the most comfortable, but I've slept in worse. As the room grows quiet, I silently tap out a message to the others to let them know I'll be unavailable because Iris is afraid to sleep alone. I expect Cat and Fran to reply with some quick comment about how they need to protect Iris from me, but no one does. Maybe Sentorr told them she was mine, and because of that, I'd never harm her. Or maybe they figured it out on their own. The thought makes me feel oddly proud. I lean back against the wall and feel the curves of my horns press against the hard surface. Not comfortable. But that doesn't matter. I listen to the steady rhythm of Iris's breathing and feel a strange sense of contentment, one I haven't felt in a really, really long time.

On the bed, Iris gasps and jerks awake. She starts to struggle under the blankets, and I immediately surge forward, touching her shoulder. I half expect her to shriek with surprise, but she goes totally still, her entire body trembling. It's almost like she's waiting for something.

"I'm here," I murmur. "You're safe, Iris."

Her body sags back against the blankets. "Alvos."

"Right here."

"I didn't know where I was." Her nostrils flare and her hand grips my wrist tightly. I notice that her silky hair is messy and the ribbon she'd carefully tied over her eyes has come loose and revealed her scars. "I thought I was back there..." She sucks in a deep breath. Another. Another, as if she's trying to calm herself with lungful after lungful. "But the air smells different. You smell different."

"That's right," I reassure her. "You're not there. You're here with me."

She takes another shuddering breath and nods, falling back against the blankets. She's beautiful and vulnerable against them, and I don't even care that the ribbon falls off of her face and exposes her scars. I wouldn't care if she ever wore that thing. She's hauntingly lovely to me and perfect in every way. The only thing I see when I see those scars are not her flaws but the bastards that did this to her. I wish I'd been the one to pull the trigger. I wish I'd been the one to see the light go out of their eyes so they knew it was for her, that I did it in her name.

I have to be content with Kivian's justice, though.

Iris tucks the blankets up to her chin and huddles underneath them. She doesn't look happy about the thought of going back to sleep. Despite the warnings not to touch her that are screaming in my brain, I reach out and brush my fingertips over her brows, smoothing her hair back from her face. "I'm here with you."

She doesn't shudder away from my touch, and I hate that I feel a sense of pleasure at that realization. Her face turns to mine and she bites her lip, then speaks. "Could you sleep with me tonight? Just so I know where I am?"

I stare at her in shock. "You trust me that much?"

"I have to trust someone," Iris whispers, and reaches out to touch my hand. "Or I think I'll fall apart."

"I won't touch you," I promise her. "I can lie on top of the blankets."

"Actually, I'd prefer that you hold me," she says, and then an uncertain look crosses her face. "But just hold me, if that's okay."

It's the first time she's demanded something instead of sweetly agreeing with whatever. I love it, and it means that she feels strongly about this. "Of course. You want me under the blankets or over?"

"Under is fine." She shivers and then pulls her hand from mine, sliding the blankets back in an invitation.

I try to ignore the response of my cock. Iris is feeling scared and vulnerable, but my cock doesn't care. It reacts to her nearness, the suggestion of those pulled back blankets and joining her in the bed. I adjust myself, tucking my length up and into my belt so it won't jut against her while she sleeps. It's painful and pinching, but I welcome that, because maybe it'll be enough of a distraction.

I hope.

10

ALYVOS

I climb into bed on the other side of her and she slides inward, moving closer to the wall. I'll be between her and the outside, and I briefly wonder if she wants to switch places, then decide that it's a deliberate choice by her. She probably feels safer wedged between a wall and my body. As carefully as I can, I lie down next to her, the only part of me brushing against her my shoulder. I can sleep like this, I decide. Stiff and uncomfortable, but close enough that she'll know I'm here with her.

Iris gives a little sigh and immediately curls up against me, pressing her cheek to my chest, her hand on my pectorals.

So much for that. I can't find it in me to object. My female's curled up in my arms. How could I ever want anything more?

A second later, she stiffens and her legs jerk up. She scuttles backward, sitting up against the head of the bed, the blankets discarded. "There's something in the bed! It touched my leg!"

Something in the bed? I pull up the covers and peer underneath. Nothing but my legs, still covered by my clothing. "There's nothing there."

"I felt something." She's trembling.

"My tail perhaps?" It brushed against her when I lay down.

"Your...tail?" Her head tilts. "You have a tail?"

"Well...yes. All mesakkah do."

Her expression still looks suspicious. "Can I touch it?"

I swallow hard. Touching a male mesakkah's tail is the equivalent of fondling his cock. She doesn't know that, though. And I don't want to admit it to her if it'll make her uncomfortable. I understand her fear, though, and I hate that I've made her worried to get into bed again. She can't see and I don't want to surprise her. "Of course."

I'm glad I managed to sound so nonchalant.

Iris slides carefully back down into the bed next to me and then reaches forward. The covers remain bunched at our feet, and I lift my tail slightly, flicking it against her hand so she knows where it is. Her fingers close on air, and I force myself to remain still when she grips it.

Ah, kef it. The moment she touches my tail, my cock presses in aching urgency against the tight pressure of my belt. I rest my flattened hand against it, determined to make it behave even as she gently explores me with both hands. Her fingers glide over the tuft of the end of my tail and then lightly move along the length of it, edging closer and closer to the sensitive base. "It's long," she murmurs. "Not what I expected when you said tail."

"No?" I sound strangled to my own ears. "What did you expect?"

Her smile is shy even as she strokes the fur of my tail, and I nearly come in my pants. "A cotton tail."

"Cotton...tail? I have no idea what that is."

"Kind of like a fuzzy bunny. You're so soft." She pets my skin. "Like a rabbit. I guess I've been picturing you as this big sort of bunny rabbit with armor. Is that weird?"

"I don't know. I'm not familiar with your planet's lifeforms. Are rabbits fierce? Warlike?"

A little giggle escapes her. "Warlike? No."

I am utterly enchanted by that small laugh. My world feels upended by the sound of her pleasure, and I know in that moment I'd do anything to hear that laughter again. Kef me, she's beautiful. I've never seen anything so perfect in my life. "That's the first time I've heard you laugh," I tell her in a husky voice.

Her expression falls, and I could punch myself for making her uncomfortable. "Haven't had much to laugh about, I'm afraid."

"I'm an idiot," I tell her. "A keffing idiot. Of course you haven't." I reach out and touch her wrist, give it a squeeze. "But I want you to know you're safe here. I'd never let anyone harm you."

She nods but doesn't answer. Maybe she doesn't believe me quite yet. She will eventually, though. It'll take time, but she'll realize I mean just what I say. I'd plow through a thousand szzt junkers to get to her if she was in danger. I'd beat ten thousand aliens with my fists. I'd do anything for her. Anything. Everything.

Iris continues to stroke my tail, and I close my eyes, determined not to let her innocent exploration make me lose control. I'd never touch her...but that doesn't mean I won't come in my pants like a schoolboy if she keeps going as she does. "Your tail is very long," she murmurs, and when she finds the base of it, she jerks away as she realizes she just brushed up against the fabric of my trou. "Oh. Sorry about that."

"It's fine," I grit out.

"I didn't mean to touch you in...such a personal way."

"You didn't," I lie. "You can touch me anywhere you want. I don't mind it." I'm just spouting words, of course, trying to make her comfortable. But when her expression turns to one of interest, I'm filled with a mixture of hot anticipation and chagrin. "Do you want to?"

"I saw a movie with a blind girl once, and she touched people's faces to learn what they looked like." Iris bites her lip, chewing on it slightly. "If it wouldn't be too intrusive, I'd like to see your face."

"Of course." I'm humbled that she wants to see who I am. That she's wondered about me. I force myself to remain completely still as she leans in with one hand, reaching out with delicate fingers.

She finds my nose first. It's prominent, like most mesakkah males'. Perhaps mine is more prominent than most. I've never given much thought to my appearance. I'm handsome enough that I get interest from females in most of the bars and cantinas we frequent, but I'm usually more focused on finding someone to fight than to mate with.

But...I hope she likes my face. I hope she doesn't find me frightening, or ugly. Cat likes Tarekh, and his face could make paint peel, so I hope my appearance doesn't offend Iris.

Light fingertips trace along my nostrils and then up the bridge of my nose, caressing each bump. Iris looks fascinated as she travels upward, to the hard crest of my brows. I know we're different here than humans. We're bony and ridged all the way up to our horns, whereas she has mobile furry little brows that let her have a hundred different expressions. She traces the ridges on my forehead and then moves down to my temples and across my eyes. I close them as she skates over my lashes and then goes down to my cheeks, then brushes my mouth.

Kef, the urge to bite those dainty fingertips is overwhelming.

Iris strokes my face, learning my jaw and then sweeping upward to my ears and then my horns. I can see the surprise on her face when she discovers them, and she caresses the bases and then slowly moves her hands all the way up. "Is this...metal?"

"Mesakkah cap our horns when we come of age. It's a sign of adulthood. Of civilization. I don't know why we do it, just that if you don't cap them, you're looked at like some sort of wild man who just emerged from the jungle on a very backwards moon."

"Wow." Her hands stroke down my hair, over the thick fall of it. "What color is this?"

"Black. My skin is blue."

Her lips part in surprise, and then she smiles shyly again. "Really? Blue? What color blue? Pale? Aqua? Dark blue?"

"Uh...just blue."

She chuckles again. "I guess I should know better than to ask a guy what shade of blue he is." Her tone is wistful. "I wish I could see it. I've never seen a blue person before."

I want to give this to her. I struggle to think of what shade it would be. "It is...the blue of a metal weapon? Like when the light hits it just right? I am not good with words."

"Oh, I think that was a wonderful description," Iris tells me, and trails her fingers through my hair before letting her hands rest on my shoulders. "And you're tall, too, aren't you? I can tell you are when I stand next to you, but with your horns you must seem giant."

"I know that you are within a handspan of Cat's height, and she does not come to my shoulder." Iris nods as if this matches her mental image, and her hands move along my shoulders, continuing their exploration. "We are broader, as well. You seem very small next to one of my people."

"You're very big," she concludes and then withdraws her hands back to her lap, as if reluctant to explore more.

I find I'm disappointed that she's done. I loved the feel of her hands on me...but I'm also glad she did not explore lower. My cock is hard and straining against my clothing, and not even the pinch of my belt is helping things. "What do you think?"

Iris gives a little sigh. "I'm afraid you're not very bunny-like after all."

"Is that bad?"

"No? In a way I'm glad you don't have whiskers and buck teeth. But you remind me of a devil like in one of the old scary stories. Your legs don't bend backward like a goat's, do they?"

Bend backward? "Why would they bend backward?"

She shrugs. "Just trying to picture the rest of you. That's what demons look like in some of our old books."

"If you want to feel my knees, you can reassure yourself that they bend the same way yours do."

"That's all right. I'll take your word for it." But the hint of a smile returns to her face and she settles down in the bed next to me. I wish she'd curl up against my chest again, but she lies next to me quietly, her face turned toward mine. "Do you find us odd looking?"

"Humans? Yes and no. When I first saw Fran and Cat, I wondered how anyone could like something so pale and puny. But now I feel differently."

"Because you know them?"

Because I know you. "Right. They're just people like everyone else. Once you get to know the person underneath, looks don't matter all that much."

She nods thoughtfully.

"Do you find me ugly? I imagine a blue male with horns and a tail is very different from what you pictured."

"If you only knew." Again, she chuckles, and I am entranced. "But no, I don't find you ugly. I'd love to see the blue, but..." She shrugs. "I'll just use my imagination." She rests her cheek on the makeshift pillow. "Thank you."

"Why are you thanking me?"

"Because you've been very kind and you don't have to be. I know I'm being needy and scared, but I appreciate you helping me."

"It is my pleasure," I tell her. I think of how calmly she lies in the bed with me. There's still so much trust that it makes me wonder. If she'd been abused sexually, would she ask for me to sleep with her? Or would our conversations be very different? "Can I ask you something?"

"Of course."

"Most slavers grab humans for a, ah, very specific sort of service. Did they...touch you?" I don't know how to say it politely.

"Did they use me for sex?" Iris shakes her head. "I think that was part of the original plan, but when they found out I was a virgin, they decided they were going to re-sell me to someone else. Some lord on an asteroid with a very long name. He wanted a human virgin. So I guess I'm lucky in that they didn't do anything...like that. I know they hurt others, though. I could hear it." Her shoulders slump and she huddles in on herself a little more. "I was very lucky."

I grunt, not sure if I agree with that statement.

"What is it?"

"You call yourself lucky and yet they hurt you terribly."

"Yes, but I could have been hurt like this and in other ways." She shrugs and tucks her hands under her cheek. "I'm alive. The others...I could hear them screaming. Dying. I could smell it." She swallows hard. "No, I'm lucky."

"Why did they cut out your eyes?"

"I was disobedient." Her tone is dull, defeated. "When they first captured me I was very angry. I struck out at everyone. Tried to steal weapons. I broke free from my cage once and sabotaged part of the ship. They'd hit me at first, but that didn't work. Neither did starving me. So they started to cut off my fingers." Her hands move together and she brushes her fingers over the missing stub of a pinky. "And I still fought back, because I didn't want to give up."

I admire her spirit...and at the same time, I wonder where it's gone. The picture she paints is a very different, feisty fighter than the calm, cringing woman at my side.

"They intended to give you away as a slave and yet they cut out your eyes? They marred you permanently? That seems like ill use of merchandise, if I'm being honest."

She shrugged. "The lord that bought me? It was his idea. He said I didn't need eyes for what he needed me for. After that..." She goes still. "I stopped fighting."

I go utterly silent. Rage blisters through my mind. There's another male to kill out there, then. Not just the two szzt that ran that junker, but this other male, this lord who thought nothing of maiming a female simply because she wouldn't behave like a docile animal.

"You're quiet," Iris says in a small voice.

"I'm angry." I hate that her shoulders stiffen. "Not at you. At the szzt that took you and hurt you. They're dead now, but I wish I could kill them all over again."

"It doesn't matter," she says softly.

It does matter. It matters a keffing lot to me. "Do you remember his name?"

"Who?"

"The lordling on the asteroid. The one who wanted a virgin." So I can keffing destroy him.

"No." She yawns and slides a little closer to me, resting her cheek against my arm. Her hands creep around my bicep, as if she wants to hold me to remind herself that she's not alone. "It was long and tongue tangling. Maybe I'd remember it if I heard it again." She shrugs.

"It doesn't matter," I tell her and caress her head, her hair sliding under my fingers like silk. "Sleep, Iris. I'll be here."

"Thank you," she whispers.

There's no need to thank me, but I leave it for now. No sense in constantly making her feel bad for politeness. No wonder there's no fight left in her. They broke her and she hasn't had time to mend.

I'll always be here for her, I decide. Always.

11

———

IRIS

I wake up in the middle of the night, disoriented. Panic flashes through me. My dreams were of carnage, of aliens with spikes that they lowered towards my eyes, gleeful looks on their ugly faces. I pant, trying to sort through my chaotic half-awake thoughts, to determine what's real and what's a dream.

Next to me, someone snores.

For some reason, that grounds me. I realize where I'm at. That there's a big, heavy arm draped over my side, pinning my arm underneath his and tucking it against my waist. Instead of making me feel trapped, I feel...safe. Comforted. I even like the snoring. I settle back down against the blankets and tuck my body closer to his.

Alvos.

He's going to keep me safe.

I go back to sleep.

12

One Week Later

IRIS

*I*t takes time for me to relax and settle in. Everything's new and strange, and I'm learning it's a lot more intimidating and very different to be blind and trapped in a small cage than blind on a strange alien ship where there are a million passageways to wander into and get lost. I start counting steps at first, until I realize that the ship's computer can give me directions, kind of like the driving app I used to have on my phone back on Earth. Space-Siri, as I call her, always stops me before I run into a wall, so I just make sure to use her as a guide until I get familiar with certain areas.

The crew talks about how small the ship is, but to me, it seems large. Bigger than a house or two slapped together. It's mostly one level, with a med-bay, a mess hall, the bridge, leisure quarters for relaxing, two storage bays, and then there are crew quarters for each of the four aliens and a maze of hallways and lockers. There's probably even more to the ship, but I haven't run into it yet. I'm not the boldest of explorers.

The crew seems nice enough. I've met all of them. The captain, Kivian, is...not what I expected. Everyone gives him shit about his clothes and his meticulousness, so I imagine him as a bit of a dandy. Fran—his human mate—is the practical one. She's level-headed and clever, and while the pirate crew did fine without her, I think she's kind of the ship mom. She makes sure everyone is taken care of and that everything's in order on the *Fool*. Tarekh's the big easygoing medic that I'm told is hideously ugly, and Cat is the ferocious and forthright human woman that's his mate. She's a pint-sized, prank-loving dervish, and I love her bold personality even if I can't mimic it.

Other than Alvos, Sentorr's the one I'm closest to, oddly enough. He's polite and reserved and doesn't feel the need to make small talk around me. He's content to sit in silence and let me just be. He doesn't have to make sure that I'm entertained at all times, like Fran does. Cat's usually attached at the hip to Tarekh, and whenever she gives a throaty little giggle, I worry that they're groping each other a few feet away from me and I can't see it. It makes it a little uncomfortable to be around them, even though I know they mean well.

Sentorr just works. He focuses on the ship and taps away at his controls on the bridge, and if I ask questions, he answers with a crisp response that has zero fluff to it. Maybe I recognize a fellow repressed person in Sentorr. I think he's like me, bottling up everything inside and giving the world a very focused picture of who he is. I'm calm and agreeable. He's efficient.

And the only people we're probably fooling are ourselves.

But still, that makes him easy to be around, unlike Alvos.

Alvos—I still call him that, still waiting to see if he corrects me —is both wonderful and difficult. I trust him implicitly at this point. He's protective and caring, doing his best to make sure that I'm comfortable and feel safe. Whenever I'm in the same room as him—which is often—he stays nearby and quietly offers me his arm in case I need a guide. He doesn't make a big deal out of it and never makes me feel like I'm a burden. Every morning, he ties the ribbon over my eyes because it makes me feel better to hide my scars from the others. And every night, he sleeps in the same bed as me with his arms curled around me. It's my favorite time of day, I think. To just settle into bed and be held tightly and know that I'm safe and cared for. We talk, too, but it's not necessary—I just like being alone with him.

Of course, he's also utterly infuriating. Alvos likes to pick fights, it seems. He's the crew's muscle, and if there's a job that needs heads knocked around or guns blazing, he's their guy. He goes with Kivian and Tarekh when they need to meet up with smugglers and usually comes back smelling faintly like blood. I'm told that it's just his nose or his knuckles, because he'd rather negotiate with his fists than with discussion. I don't mind this—but I do mind that he's sometimes trying to pick a fight with me. He goads me, trying to make me snap back at him. He snarls when I thank him. He does small things all day long to try and prick my temper, to get me to show something other than placidity.

But I learned that lesson already. Placidity is safe. Being as feisty as Cat cost me my eyes, half a pinky, and a toe. I can't do that anymore.

So I just ignore when he growls at me when I'm polite. I ignore the little verbal nudges he gives me in effort to make me lose my temper. I'm calm and unruffled, sweet and polite, even when I don't want to be.

It makes him crazy. I think he'd like it if I was wild and out of control, but I can't do that. I can't be that girl anymore.

The only part of me that's left is the obedient one.

I do my best to help out with the crew, though I can't do much. I don't know how to operate any of the ship's equipment. I can't read alien languages. I have a translation chip thanks to Tarekh's medical wizardry, but it only helps with spoken languages. There's not a lot for a blind girl to do, and it makes me feel guilty. Everyone has a job on ship, it seems. Fran takes inventory regularly and helps Kivian with various duties around the ship. Cat helps Tarekh with maintenance. Sentorr apparently lives at his nav station. Alvos is in charge of weaponry.

I can't really do much with weaponry because I can't see, and I can't leave the ship to help him "muscle" their contacts. I don't want to leave the ship, either. Not when I'm safe here. So I hang out on the bridge with Sentorr and try to stay out of people's way.

It's a busy week, it seems. Kivian and the others are meeting with smugglers at a space station and setting up a series of recurring shipments of something called "darkmatter." It seems that the *Fool's* crew finds buyers, goes to dangerous locations on the outer reaches of the planetary system and bargain/steal the stuff they need, and then mark it up for a ridiculous price to sell back. I get the impression that they lie, steal and cheat if necessary, but they're a tight crew and they're good people at heart, so it actually doesn't bother me that they're breaking the law. I've listened to how Tarekh and Kivian take care of their women and there's no evil in these people's hearts.

I'm not much help to a pirate crew, though. Eventually, Sentorr gets tired of me sitting quietly on the bridge with my hands folded in my lap and doing nothing. He moves to the station I'm sitting at and starts to tap at buttons on the panel in front of me—

a panel that I don't dare touch because I don't know what it does. While the others are at the cantina wheeling and dealing, he shows me how to work the comm panels without sight, how many taps of this button get me to the menu I need, and then he gives me a strangely shaped earpiece that just barely manages to go into my ear.

"Listen for the authorities," he tells me. "These are the local comm channels that the police and militia in this system use to communicate. If you hear that they're mobilizing, let me know. If you hear anything out of the ordinary, you tell me. Don't be afraid to speak up."

"All right," I tell him in a timid voice, and listen to the radio frequencies and messages.

At first, it's just boring. There's a lot of chatter about setting up at routine stops and switching out of guardsmen at established hours. After a while, though, I start to enjoy it. I flip through several of the comm bands, and I find that the hours fly past. I enjoy listening in because it tells me where the police are that particular day. If they're doing routine checks on the station or if they've hit their quota for the month and are easing back. I hear the militia griping about unregistered vehicles in their territory and we know not to steer the *Fool* toward one particular planet because they're cracking down.

After about two days of flipping through channels, I overhear news of a freighter in a nearby shipping lane that's been abandoned, the crew jettisoning in life pods toward the closest station. I share this with Alvos and the others, and the next thing I know, we're setting a course for it. Hours later, the cargo—guns, it seems —has been offloaded into the *Fool's* berth and we're speeding away. Kivian and others pat my back and tell me that I've just earned the *Fool* money. Fran comments how helpful it is to have me listening to the radio, since it's gotten them into trouble before.

I feel good. Useful. Like I can do something other than be a victim. I hope it's enough to earn me a place here.

Because I'm not sure I have a place anywhere else.

13

ALYVOS

*I*ris's unflappable calm is driving me insane.

I glare at my drink in the mess hall as the others celebrate. We're all together—even Sentorr has abandoned his post on the bridge to come and join in the merrymaking for a time. He sits next to Iris, watching with amusement as Cat needles Tarekh, her arms around the big male's neck and leaning over his shoulder as he drinks a sip of her beverage and then makes a face.

"It tastes like piss," he declares. "Humans drink this voluntarily?"

"It's beer, and yes they do." Cat licks his earlobe, grinning. "And you have to down the whole thing."

He gives me a mock-pained look. I just glare at my own beer. We found a crate of these on the abandoned freighter, along with packaged snacks from another Class D world that look like bugs of some kind. Fran suspects there's some kind of upsell on the black market for these sorts of things. We decided to keep the beer and celebrate, since that freighter's cargo will now buy us a month's fuel as well as some other things. Kivian and Fran are beaming at Iris for being clever enough to pick up the alert. Even Sentorr's giving her a proud look.

And Iris just sits there with her hands clasped in her lap, as cool and unruffled as ever, the red ribbon covering her eyes, the unflappable hint of a smile on her mouth.

The last week has been both bliss and hell. Having Iris in my life makes everything better. I love waking up in the morning and seeing her lying there next to me. I love the scent of her. I love the feel of her body in my arms and the way she burrows against me. I love her rare chuckles and her rarer true smiles.

This day should be a day of celebration as she finds her spot with us. As she gets comfortable and the question of whether or not she should stay turns into a formal welcome into the *Fool's* ranks. Instead, the others celebrate around her, not noticing that her expression is as carefully blank as ever.

But I notice. I notice everything about her.

I also notice Sentorr is sitting right next to her and that she's been spending more and more time on the bridge with him.

I shouldn't care. He knows she's mine. He's not indicated to me any interest other than friendship.

Doesn't mean I like it when he smiles in her direction. Or when Fran mentions that Iris should spend even more time on the bridge picking through comms to find us other abandoned freighters. I'm jealous. It's not logical, but nothing about how I feel for Iris is logical.

I want her smiles to be for me.

More than that, I want her smiles to be real. Then I'll know she's no longer living in fear. Until then, I hate every apology she makes, every gracious gesture. Every quiet moment. They all make me crazy with frustration.

I know it's only been a week, but I'm desperate to see changes in her. To know that someday she'll be happy and comfortable. To be less broken than she is now. I want her to realize that this is her home.

That I am, too.

I'm an impatient bastard, though. I know it's early. I know she needs time. I just want her to reach for me when she's struggling. Maybe that's selfish of me, but I'm already crazy with need for her.

And all I get are the same patient, distant smiles that the others get.

I scowl at my beer, beyond frustrated.

"You feeling all right today?" Fran asks me, curious. She's caught my surly expression and is looking at me with concern.

I shrug, wondering if Iris will notice, and then I decide I'm being childish. Pouting to see if the girl pays attention to me? I'm a keffing fool. "Just distracted."

"Someone wasn't his usual self on the ship," Cat comments, reaching over Tarekh's shoulder to grab his beer and take a sip. "You didn't even look sad that there wasn't anyone to punch out."

I shrug again. She's not wrong. Normally my bloodthirst rages the moment we board another ship. Doesn't matter if there's not anyone there. I go into "battle mode," ready to fight at a second's notice. Today, I wasn't in the mood, though. I kept wondering if Iris was all right, if she was worried that I wasn't at her side.

I mostly just wanted to get back to her.

I could still take down anyone that came after us, of course. I just wasn't as hungry for it today as I normally am. It seems my lust for violence has been replaced by a different kind of lust.

I glance over at Iris. She's turned towards me, but that passive, fake smile's on her lips, and it just makes my mood worse. I get to my feet. "I'm just not feeling it today." I leave the room before anyone else can comment. I know I'm being a jerk, but I'm not in the right mindset this night for light-hearted joking and I don't want to bring everyone else down.

I wish I was more patient. I'm not like Tarekh, who gave Cat all the space she needed and waited months and months for her to come to him. If it takes Iris years to come to me...I might go mad first. It'll be worth it, but I'll still be crazed until then. I hope this ship is ready to have a cranky member on board, I think to myself rather sourly as I head into the quarters I share with Iris.

Being there alone feels strange, though. I sit on the edge of the bed and rub my chin, contemplating "my" room. Our room, really. Ever since that first night, she hasn't asked me not to sleep with her. In fact, every night just before bed, she crawls under the covers and reaches for me, like it's implied that we're going to sleep together that night. And of course I want that. Holding my female against me for hours and hours? Keeping her in my arms and knowing that she feels safe there? There's no feeling in the world quite like it. I've never tried to touch her or to push her for the kisses the humans love so much. It doesn't seem right.

Maybe my impatience isn't that I want to make Iris mine—kisses and mating and all—so much as that I want her real personality to spark. I want the real Iris to show up. When someone makes a shitty comment, I want her to reach over and smack them in the mouth like Fran or Cat would.

I might be asking too much from her, though. She's a broken thing, like me. Survival is still first and foremost on her mind, and this is how Iris has chosen to survive.

I rub the plates on my brow and wish that I was a better male for her, a more understanding one. I understand her broken parts, but that doesn't mean that I know how to handle them.

The door to my room chimes. "Iris," it calls out, and a moment later the object of my desires enters the room, her hand on the wall. Her head moves back and forth, as if searching the room for me. "Alvos?"

"I'm here." I gaze at her achingly lovely face and feel need gnawing at me. "You should rejoin the others. I'm foul company tonight."

She hesitates. Part of me hopes that she tosses her hair and sits down next to me anyhow. At least that'd be defiance. But she remains in the doorway, as if even that small act is too much for her. "Is everything all right?"

I want to say yes just so she'll let it go, but I never want to lie to her. "It's a long story."

"I like stories," Iris says in a soft voice. "And I'm a good listener."

I grunt but don't offer more than that.

Her head tilts. "Is it me? Are you mad at me?"

"I'm not real happy with you right now, no. But that's my problem."

I watch as she sucks in a breath. "What did I do to offend you?" Her words are stated like a problem to be solved. "Can you tell me so I won't do it again?"

For a moment, I want to tell her that she's fine. That it's me that's the problem. But my frustration bubbles up and I get up from the bed, approaching her where she stands in the doorway. I'm glad to see that she doesn't flinch back, but I still need more from her. "You really want to know?"

"I do."

"I need you to show me something. Anything. I need emotion from you."

She's very still. "Emotion?"

"Anything," I snarl, leaning in. I'm taking it out on her, I know. I just hate that she's so keffing calm. "Anger. Frustration. Pissiness. Something more than just smiling like everything in the world is all right with you when it's not. Being mad when someone cuts your keffing eyes out—"

She slaps me. Her hand darts out so fast and quick that I'm surprised she even moved. Of course, she's smaller than I am so her hand smacks my chin more than my cheek.

We're both stunned into silence. The air hangs heavy between us for a long moment.

I laugh, the sound rumbling up from my belly. I'm thrilled.

Iris has a different reaction. She begins to tremble all over, her body quaking. Her face has gone utterly pale and she looks ready to collapse. "I'm sorry," she says quickly, and her voice is shaky. "I'm so sorry—"

"It's all right," I begin, but her trembling continues. "Shhh," I whisper, cupping her face in my hands. I'm immediately full of chagrin. I hate that she's so terrified. I wanted the response, but not if it costs her this fear. "I'm the one that should apologize. I've picked fights for too long looking for it to settle something inside me. You're not the one I should be picking a fight with."

"I'm sorry," she whispers again, her shivering unstoppable. "I just...I can't. I'm scared. Being blank like that...it's safe."

"I don't want you to be safe with me, Iris," I murmur. Her mouth is so lovely and so close that I want to brush my thumb over it. I want to lean over and put my lips over hers to try one of those human kisses that look so strange but seem so enjoyable for both parties. "I want you to be who you truly are with me. Not who you think I want. Not the person you feel is least objectionable."

"I'm not there yet," she whispers, and her hands go to cover mine. She clings to me. "Please don't hate me for it."

I groan low in my throat. "I could never hate you, Iris. Never. Don't even let the thought cross your mind." I stroke my thumbs over her cheeks. "You're not ready yet, but when you are, I'll be waiting here for my punch to the face."

She chuckles, just a little. It's not quite enough, but it'll do.

14

IRIS

*T*hat night, I slide closer to Alvos in the bed we share. After he left the little party, the mood changed and it was hard for me to stay with the others. They went on celebrating and didn't seem to be surprised that Alvos picked a fight—that's apparently his thing—but my mind stayed with him even when my body didn't.

It's funny how no matter how hard I pretend, he still sees right through me. He knows I'm not this calm, docile person I pretend to be. How much I'm burying underneath. But I'm also terrified of being the person I used to be. The one that would sass without a thought to how it'd be received. That if you didn't like it, that was your problem.

That woman had her eyes, though. I'm not the same and never will be.

And yet, I want to be who Alvos wants me to be. I want to be unafraid. God, I want that more than anything. I put my hand on his chest and feel bare skin and the bony plates on his breast. Sometime in the last week, he's stopped wearing a shirt to bed. He still wears his pants, and even though he gives me space, I can sometimes feel the prodding heat of his cock against my back-side. It doesn't scare me, because he never touches me inappro-priately. Every time his hands are on me, they are tender and respectful. He's never grabbed my breasts or between my thighs like the other aliens did.

I know he wants more from me because I think he wants me as his mate. I'm not that clueless or naïve. There's an electric sort of attraction between us, and he wouldn't care if I answered him blandly if he didn't want more.

Truth is…I might want something like that, too. I lean in closer to him and breathe deep of his scent. He smells so good, and I'm addicted to touching him. I love how safe he makes me feel, and how strong he is. I love his personality, even when he's being prickly or pushing me too hard.

But I'm scared, and I'm worried to make that leap. I don't know if my head's in the right place just yet to be looking at a relation-ship, especially one with an alien. I don't trust myself, so I need to take things slow.

It doesn't mean I'm not tempted, too. But I don't trust myself yet.

15

Weeks Later

ALYVOS

*J*ris and I have fallen into a good routine, I think.

At least, it's good for me. I'm pretty sure she likes it, too. We sleep together every night. She's a surprisingly calm sleeper. I thought for sure she'd have nightmares—I know I did for years after the war—but as long as she can hold on to me, she sleeps well.

I love that she holds on to me, so I don't mind in the slightest. It means we wake up most mornings twined around each other, and when her clothes are pushed up and expose her oddly-colored skin, I have to fight back the urge to fling her down on the bed and kef the daylights out of her.

I don't, of course. I want her to feel safe.

This morning, she gets out of bed and stretches, the tunic pulling taut over her breasts, and I furtively palm my cock. It doesn't matter that she can't see me doing it—it still feels wrong to touch myself with her standing right there, unaware. Iris rubs her hair absently and then heads toward the water closet, one hand out in front of her. "Coming?" she asks me sleepily.

I wish. I know that's not what she's asking, though, and so I fight back my urges. "Coming."

She showers and then wraps herself in towels, heading to the main part of my chamber while I jump in and take a quick shower myself. There's time enough to jerk my cock to a silent, brutal completion, and then I soap up and rinse off speedily before heading out to dress.

Iris is waiting, dressed in a jumper, and holds the comb out to me when I approach. "If you don't mind," she murmurs.

I never mind. This is part of our routine, and I love brushing out her silky hair for her. I take my time, carefully detangling wet strands. After everything is combed and neat, I'll put it in a braid for her. I tie it with another ribbon borrowed from Cat, though it's looking a little sad and worn at the use it's gotten. I finish her braid and then stroke it lightly before laying it on her shoulder. "You need more ribbons and hair clasps. I'll get you some when we dock at the station later today."

"Thank you," she says evenly.

I wish she'd have more of a response than a mild platitude. But Iris is always sweet and easygoing. She never minds anything. She's never upset. She never asks for anything at all—not extra hot water for the shower, or a larger towel, or a bigger pillow. She never asks for a single thing.

It makes me crazy.

I toy with the end of her braid as she sits calmly in front of me.

"Can I ask you something?" I know I'm probably picking a fight, but I can't help myself. I want a response out of her. Something. Anything.

"Of course."

"One of the first things both Cat and Fran asked for when they got on the *Fool* was to go home. Back to Earth. You've never even brought it up. How come?" She opens her mouth to speak, and before she can, I interrupt. "And don't tell me it's because you don't feel like going home. I know that's not true."

Iris struggles for a moment with her answer, and when she speaks, her voice is thick with emotion. "I haven't asked, no. I guess after...things happened, I knew I'd never go home again." She swallows hard and toys with her fingers—rubbing over the amputated one, I notice. "Has that changed?"

"No," I say harshly. And then I feel like a keffing asshole because I'm the one that brought it up and made her sad. "There's no going back to Earth."

I'm frustrated by her small, accepting nod. It makes me feel worse than ever. How can I love her and want to shake her at the same time? But I do.

She's so calm. I want her to be a thunderstorm. A flurry of anger. I'd rather that she was chaos and rage and tears, because those I could understand.

This unnatural placidity? I don't understand that at all.

16

IRIS

"*A*ll right, someone give me a verb." I hear Fran's fingers tapping on her tablet.

"Dicking," Cat says with a giggle.

I snicker a bit at that, too, lifting my mug to my lips. The hot tea that they prefer on this ship isn't quite coffee, but it suits the need easily enough. I'm pretty sure the others are drinking more of the beer, but I'm like the mesakkah—I don't have the taste for it.

"Everything's dick to you," Fran teases her.

"God, yeah," Cat replies dreamily. "I love me some dick."

This time they both giggle, and I'm smiling, too. The *Fool* is docked at a station for refueling, and Kivian is off playing a gambling game called "sticks." Part of the pirate crew's plans is to show up at different stations, toss money around like they're careless high rollers, and then reel them in the next time they show up. Part of the game is playing people, and that's the part Kivian's fantastic at. Alvos and Tarekh hang out at a nearby table and run interference.

Since there's no one on the ship but us ladies and Sentorr, we decide to have a game night. Of course, I can't see to play sticks, which involves careful placement of colors and game pieces. The girls also have playing cards and dominos, but I can't play cards and my memory's not good enough for dominos. So we started with crosswords and drinking, and now we've progressed to a mesakkah game called Choices, which is pretty much just the alien version of Mad Libs. It's apparently huge on Homeworld, Fran says. At any rate, it's fun.

And it's really funny when you get a few beers into Cat. She makes every word completely filthy. At least half of them every time are "dick." Or some form of "dick."

"We need a noun," Fran says.

"Diiiiick," Cat calls out. "All the dick!"

"Girl, lay off the beer. Let Iris play a little."

"Dick, Iris," Cat whispers, leaning toward me. Her breath fans over my cheek and it definitely smells like beer. "Tell her dick."

"How about tea?" I take another sip of mine and lift my cup to indicate.

Cat groans. "God, you are no fun. Sentorr has better words than you. We should ask him to do the next one."

"Good idea," Fran says, and I hear her click on the comm. "Hey, Sentorr. Are you busy?" Cat giggles drunkenly and I'm totally amused by what a lightweight she is. I wasn't sure about playing games with the others—I'm still cautious and reserved around them—but I have to admit that this is a lot of fun.

"What can I help you with, Fran?" Sentorr asks, oh so polite. His voice is tinny over the comm.

"Can you give me an adjective? A describing word? Like 'fast' or 'blue' or something."

"Are you playing Choices?" Is that amusement I hear in his voice?

"We are. Adjective, please?"

"Mm, let me think. I'm quite good at this game, you know." Cat gives a little snort, but Sentorr must not hear it. A moment later, he answers. "How about 'stiff'?"

"Thank you," Fran chokes out. I hear the comm click off, and then a moment later, both women are howling with laughter.

"Stiff!" Cat shrieks, giggling. "Oh my god! This is amazing."

I smile into my tea. "He did say he was good at this game."

They just erupt into more laughter. "This is the filthiest story ever," Fran says, wheezing and laughing. "I love it. We totally have to share this with the guys when they get back." She sighs happily and then taps on her tablet again. "Okay, where were we? It's your turn, Cat."

"Hit me," Cat says loudly. "I'm ready for it!"

"Noun."

"Dick." Cat erupts into giggles.

Fran sighs. "You've already used 'dick' this time, nerd. Pick something else. Iris, you want to take this one?"

"Oh, I'm good," I tell her and just smile. I'd much rather listen to their banter than offer up much of my own. I'm still not comfortable enough to laugh and joke and drink with them, but I do enjoy being around it. I wish Alvos was here, though. I wonder what he'd pick for a noun. Maybe "braid"? Just this morning he braided my hair for me again. Usually he comments on how soft it is and how he likes to touch it. I get a little flushed thinking about it, and then I remember that this morning we talked about Earth and I got the impression that he was frustrated with me.

It makes me sad, but I don't know what to do. I want him to like me.

I want him to like me a lot.

As the days pass, I find myself more and more drawn toward him. It's not just that he's protective and caring. He seems to understand what I'm going through, and if he pushes me sometimes, it's because he wants me to stop being so afraid. I get that. I want to stop being so afraid, too. I'm just not sure I can.

No one's ever made me feel so safe and cared for, though. The others talk about how hot-tempered Alvos is, but all I know is that he's utterly kind and patient. He's got a wry sense of humor and a stubborn streak a mile long. He holds me tenderly every night and never tries to force me into anything. Sometimes I wish he'd say something about his nightly erection that we both know he sports, but he never does. It's like my needs supersede his, and while that's sweet...sometimes I wonder what it'd be like if he threw me down on the bed and passionately kissed the heck out of me.

Okay, I wonder about the kissing a lot. Like daily. Every time he touches me. Every time his breath fans over my skin while we sleep. If I was bold like Cat, or confident like Fran, I'd grab him by the collar and show him how humans kiss. But...I just can't. Something in me locks up at the thought and then I'm frozen in place. That I'm going to encourage him and he'll change on me.

That I'll end up back in a cage, and it'll be my fault when they start taking pieces of me again.

Alvos seems to understand my hesitation. There have been a few times that we've brushed against each other in the tight quarters of his room when things felt...charged between us. When his touches might linger a little longer than they should. Maybe if I had my sight I wouldn't notice it, but when I'm down a sense, all the touches become that much more meaningful.

And yet he's still the perfect gentleman. He holds me close and helps me when I need eyes. He talks for hours when I wake up from a nightmare, simply so I can hear another person's voice and know that I'm not caged. He's a good man.

A man I could love, if I'd let myself.

"For real," Fran says, her words slightly slurred. "Give me a noun. And not 'dick.'"

"Spur," Cat replies.

They both snicker.

"Spur?" I ask absently, stirring my tea with a small spoon. "What's that?"

Both women howl with laughter.

I wait for the laughter to finish, wondering what it is I missed. I feel left out of the joke, and that sucks.

Of course, any hurt I feel disappears when the giggles just keeps going on and on. Cat starts wheezing and gasping, and Fran's little bubbles of laughter turn into breathless protests of "I can't, I can't, I can't."

Whatever it is, they're having a great time. They're also drunk as skunks, which is funny, too. I like hearing their light-hearted amusement. It almost feels like having friends again...which is ironic, because even now I hold myself apart from the others. I'm not drinking. I'm not sharing in the fun with abandon. I'm here but...I'm not.

Story of my life lately.

I get to my feet and take my teacup to the sink. The cups here are foreign feeling in my hands, and the sink is an odd shape, but some things don't change no matter the technology. It feels comfortable to press my hand against the cool metal counter, and then I turn and smile at the others, hiding my feelings. "I think I'll check in on Sentorr and see how he's doing. I hate that he's all alone on the bridge."

Cat snort-giggles. "That's how he likes it."

She's probably not wrong, but there's something comfortable about his silence. I like sitting with him. "Maybe I'll see if he wants some tea." I feel around until I find one of the mugs, then place it under the dispenser. I let my fingers wander over the buttons, feeling for the one that's been pressed so many times that it's been worn through and feels a little rougher against my fingertip. That's the one for the tea. I hit the button and then wait for the dispenser to make the tiny little click that tells me it's done, and then I pick it up and cradle it in my hands. I'm getting better at finding my way around, but it's still a process. I wave to the others and head for the bridge.

"All right, give me another noun," Fran says between chuckles as I slip out of the room.

I count steps carefully, heading toward the bridge. I keep one hand out in front of me as I walk, and I move very slowly. After over a week of learning the *Fool*, I know how many steps there are to the bridge, how many to med-bay, how many to Alvos's quarters, and every other path I go on regularly. It's a lot of memorizing, and I have to concentrate because if I get distracted or lose track, I can quickly end up running into a wall. When Alvos is here, he offers me an arm or acts as my guide, and while I like the attention—and his company—I also want to be more independent. It's crucial that I learn to get around without relying on someone.

Thirty-seven steps, a right turn, and then another twenty-two steps and I wave my hand in front of the wall panel that leads to the bridge. "Iris," the computer announces as the door opens, and I step inside.

I wait a moment, getting my bearings. The bridge is silent, and I mentally map things out. Ten steps to the right is Alvos's terminal, and a few steps beyond that is Sentorr's navigation terminal. There's a big screen at the front, and Kivian—or Fran—sits there from time to time. There's another booth for comm and miscellaneous tasks, and that's "unofficially" Tarekh's spot, though Cat tells me he doesn't do much on the bridge except heckle Sentorr.

The navigator grunts, acknowledging my presence.

I lift the tea. "Brought you a drink."

"Not that beer, I hope," he says. He doesn't get up to take it from my hands, which I appreciate in a roundabout sort of way. It'd be easier for me if he did, but I need to stop thinking about what's easy and start thinking about long-term independence. So I count steps and move forward, and when my hand falls on the edge of the desk at his station, I feel a sense of accomplishment.

I hold the tea out. "Not beer. I don't think there'll be much left when Cat and Fran get done." I offer him an easy smile. "Just tea."

There's a tug on the mug in my hand, and I wait until I'm positive that he has it before I let go. "Drunk, are they?"

"More silly than drunk, I think, but give it a few more hours." I turn and move toward Alvos's station, trying to touch as few things as possible. I don't want to accidentally hit an "eject" button or something terrible like that. Alvos reassures me that there's no such thing, but I still worry about that. I find Alvos's chair and sit down at the station. There's a small listening device I can unplug from the panel and attach to my ear, and as I do, I flick on the comm. Lately it's been soothing and kind of fun to listen through all of the conversations going on in deep space and to try and find one that might lead to something the crew can pirate. There's a couple of comm bands used by shipping lane enforcement near certain stations or planets, and I flip through those regularly. Some of the arguments go over my head despite the translator in my ear, because I don't know some of the things discussed. I don't know ship parts, or certain items that are being towed, but I do know to listen for engine trouble, or cargo issues, or stolen vehicles. Some things are universal.

I flick on the band and settle in comfortably, listening to the alien chatter. This one sounds like a warning for a traffic stop of some kind, and it amuses me how much things stay the same even in deep space and alien cultures. I think for a moment of the conversation with the girls earlier, and then pull the ear piece out. "Hey, Sentorr?"

"What?" He's abrupt, but not in a rude way, I don't think. He sounds distracted. Like I'm breaking his concentration.

"What's a spur?"

It's utterly quiet on the bridge. So quiet, I wonder if I've said something offensive. Then I hear Sentorr take in a deep, deep breath, so loud I can hear him suck in air. "I am not going to answer that," he says in the stiffest voice I've ever heard.

I can feel my cheeks heat. Yeah, it's dirty, just like I suspected. "Sorry. Someone mentioned it and...never mind."

He makes a strangled sound. "Ask Alyvos if you must."

"I'll do that," I murmur and put the earpiece back in. Like heck I will. Things are awkward enough between us without me asking what a spur is. I'm sure it's some sort of sex thing based off of how Fran and Cat howled with laughter. I'm also pretty sure Alvos would answer me as best he could without making things weird. But things are already...tense between us.

No, I think to myself as I turn the comms up and listen absently to the chatter. "Tense" isn't the right way to describe it. Maybe "fraught." Or..."anticipation." Something along those lines. "Tense" makes it sound like things are bad, and things are actually really, really good. I'm attracted to him in all kinds of ways that I probably shouldn't be. I think about him and his mouth when we sleep in bed together, and wonder what it'd be like to kiss him. I wonder if he thinks about touching me like I constantly think about touching him.

Of course, I always come up with excuses for touching him, because I can't quite resist. I'll hold on to his arm when I don't need to, or slide a bit closer in bed. He still showers with me, because the silence in the bathroom terrifies me. I don't know what it is about that small room, but as soon as the water comes on and drowns out my hearing, I panic. He stays with me and talks to keep me company, and I suspect I could probably try to shower on my own at this point because I need to work on being independent...but I don't want to. Part of me loves the thought of him watching me soap up. It turns me on even though I'd never admit it to him.

Half the time I'm not even sure I want to admit it to myself. I feel like I shouldn't be attracted to him. Like the last thing I should be thinking about right now is sex.

But oh god, is it EVER the first thing on my mind. I'm just so entranced by how caring and protective he is. How big and strong and curiously gentle with me, which seems to surprise everyone because he's known for his bad temper and like of picking fights. He's not like that with me at all. I've never felt unsafe around him. That's part of my worry—that I feel so safe around him I'm attaching feelings I shouldn't be having. I can't trust my own judgment. How much time has to pass before I can, though? Will I ever? Or am I always going to be traumatized?

I remember what he told me when I first arrived—that I'll never get over being "broken." I'll just get better at it. He's right. I wonder if it's okay to be broken in this way or if he'd think badly of me. I wish I knew.

Absently, I turn my thoughts to the comms as something familiar pings. I pause the comm-scanner on the channel I'm on and listen in to the conversation.

"When's the shipment due?" someone asks in an alien language that sounds very familiar.

17

IRIS

*I*t takes me a moment, but then I recognize the sounds, the harsh, unpleasant-to-the-ear tones of the alien language. It's the language of the orange aliens that kidnapped me. My skin prickles and I want to turn the channel.

But I don't.

"You know the lord is angry and wants his toys soon," one says.

"I know. We're working on it."

"The lord wants to know if there are any virgins," the first one hisses. "He's still angry about the last one going missing."

My skin prickles with awareness, my breath speeding up.

"There's a handful of them. There's bound to be one that hasn't had her cunt ripped apart by every alien dick in the sector." A crude laugh. "Or you want me to personally check them out?"

"I don't care what you do. I'm just saying that the lord will pay double for a virgin. A docile one. He doesn't like it when they fight."

"He's missing out, then. That's half the fun." More crude laughter.

I feel like I'm choking. Like there's not enough air in the ship. Heck, in the entire universe. They haven't said a name. I need to hear a name before I completely freak out. I don't remember the lord's name exactly, but I'd know it if I heard it. Besides, how many lords are there out in the universe looking to buy virgins?

But maybe I'm wrong. Maybe I'm hearing things that aren't necessarily true, that it's all in my head and I'm just piecing things together from my past experience. They might not even be talking about humans.

"Does he have a preference?"

"A preference for what?"

"They come in different colors. Brown, pale pink, or that ugly pasty shade that looks like they lived in a cave all their lives. And the hair—yellow hair? Orange hair? Black hair? No hair?"

"Mmm, what do you got?"

A laugh barks through the line, and I jump in my seat at how loud and rough it is. "Friend, I can make whatever he wants happen. If he likes them with yellow hair, they'll have yellow hair."

The other laughs. "Just as long as they're docile."

"Oh, they'll be docile by the time they get to him, never fear."

Goosebumps prickle up and down my arms. I feel sick. They still haven't mentioned a name and I'm growing more anxious by the moment, because I need to hear it. I don't know what I'll do if I confirm it, but I have to find out the answer for my own peace of mind.

The first one grunts. "Give me a few days to arrange things. You'll be in Sector 7 at the arranged meeting place?"

"Of course. Bring your cargo and I'll bring your pay."

"Will do. Give Lord Unto'Abarri'Nil Vohs Bekhinto, Lord of Nine Sunrises and Ruler of the Thirteenth Moon my regards."

"Learned all his names, eh?"

"Naturally."

"Ass licker," the other says with amusement. "I'll tell him you're bringing his toys." He terminates the comm.

I hit the button on the panel that'll notate the time and frequency of the comm and then rip my earpiece out. I'm panting as if I ran a mile, and there's a cold sweat on my body.

"Everything all right?" Sentorr asks in that distracted voice of his. Probably isn't even looking up from his panel.

"Just…a headache. Think I'll skip listening for now." I just need to get away from this. From the thought of Lord Unto-whatever buying more virgins. More docile girls that he can use and abuse. More girls that might have their eyes gouged out because they're bad at obeying like I was.

I don't know what to do with this information. I think about passing it along to Alvos and the others, but the thought terrifies me. What if they go after him and something bad happens? What if Lord Unto-blahblah kills them? Imprisons them? Catches them and finds me?

I retreat off the bridge, stumbling down the hall toward the chamber I share with Alvos. I run into a wall and smack my shoulder hard, but I don't care. I just need to get away. For once, the quiet of my chamber will feel good. It'll be a place I can hide away from things instead of a place that traps me. I slap my hand against the panel several times, my entire body shaking with terror and anxiety. I think of the aliens that held me down, that brought their knives toward my eyes and laughed when I screamed. "This wasn't our idea," one told me in a mocking, cold voice. "Lord's orders."

Lord Unto doesn't think of humans as people. We're just things to be bought and broken in, like horses. He wants a bunch of docile animals for his stable. I loathe the idea. I should tell the others what's happening, let them swoop in and teach Lord Unto a lesson. Steal the other girls away from him.

But...what if something goes wrong and I end up back in his hands? I push through the door of Alvos's room as it opens and move toward the bed, nearly falling over it in my haste. I crawl under the covers and pull them over my head, but that doesn't stop my shaking. I still don't feel safe. I rub the end of my cut-off pinky and touch the scars under my ribbon. Is he doing this to someone else? Hurting them like how they hurt me because I didn't matter? Because I wasn't a person in their eyes?

How do I let this continue?

But...everything's going so well here. I feel safe for the first time in ages. Even if I'm still learning how to be useful, the others are kind and friendly. I like Fran and Cat. I could be happy here.

I could be happy with Alvos. I could love him. He sees the broken parts of me and doesn't care.

Now that I've heard that comm, though, I'm going to worry about who else is trapped with him...and if I can be brave enough to ask the others to rescue them. Or if I'm going to be selfish and say nothing at all.

I don't know what to do.

18

ALYVOS

We get back from the cantina late. I stink of smoke and bubblers, but I'm still eager to see Iris. I've missed her tonight, and even though I normally love a day in the cantina—because someone's always bound to get into a brawl in a space station bar—I found myself impatient to get back to her side. To tell her about the things I saw that day and hear her thoughts. To just listen to her voice or curl up in bed around her and talk of unimportant things. I like just being with her, and hours away from her feel like wasted time.

When we get back on board the *Fool*, though, Cat and Fran are both drunk and passed out on one of the rec room couches, a tablet tucked under Fran's chest and both females with empty beer bottles scattered around them. Both Kivian and Tarekh find this incredibly amusing, and scoop up their mates, carrying them off to bed. I check for Iris on the bridge, since I know she prefers Sentorr's quiet company over being alone, but she's not there.

Huh. I find her in my chamber, huddled in the bed with the covers pulled over her head, sleeping restlessly. As I watch, she turns over in the bed and makes an unhappy noise, kicking the blankets off her feet. Normally she sleeps so quietly. Maybe she drank some of the beer, too.

A protective surge of affection washes through me as I gaze at her sleeping form. I can't wait to pull her in my arms and just feel her body against mine. To wake up with her and talk about the day before. To breathe in her scent and the sight of her like a besotted, lovesick fool—the ship's new name is an apt one, it seems. Amused by my own thoughts, I head into the water closet to rinse off the cantina stink before I get into bed with her.

I get out a few moments later to see her still moving under the blankets. Her mouth is pulled down in a frown, and there's a sheen of sweat on her body. She lets out a whimper as I approach, and her head thrashes on the pillow I got for her.

A nightmare. A bad one, it seems. I crouch quietly by the bed, unsure if I should wake her or let it play out and hope it subsides. She's still easily spooked, my lovely Iris.

I can't stand to see her suffer, though, even in her dreams. I kneel beside her and touch her arm. She cries out, flinching backward, obviously terrified.

"It's me," I whisper. "You're having a nightmare."

Her face grows tense, and for a moment it looks as if she's about to sob. Then she grabs my arm tightly and runs her hand up and down my arm. A sigh of relief escapes her. "Fuzzy skin. It's you."

"I'm here," I tell her. "You're safe."

I'm hoping that my reassurance calms her, but she still looks distraught. "Not safe. Nowhere's safe," she mumbles, pushing her hair out of her face as she sits up.

"You're wrong." I sit on the bed next to her and rub her arm, trying to soothe her fears. She sometimes has nightmares, but she's always so very self-contained when she wakes up. Tonight, she's distraught. I've always said that I'd rather see real, genuine emotion from her, but I've been lying to myself. I hate seeing her like this. I hate that she's terrified and I can't do anything to ease that fear. "I'd never let anything happen to you. You're mine."

The moment the words leave my mouth, they seem to hang out there in the air. Of course she's mine. As the days have passed and she's woken up in my arms every morning, it's just reaffirmed what I've always felt—that Iris is mine and she's meant to be my mate. I've just never told her such a thing for fear of scaring her... but I can't take it back now. In a way, I'm glad it's said. Now she knows how I feel.

But now I've given her yet another thing to be afraid of.

Her hands move up my arm, feeling her way. They go to my shoulders and then she puts them on my face, touching my jaw.

I remain still because if she wants to explore me, I welcome it. I love her touch, and I crave the moments that she reaches out for me. It makes me hope that someday things won't be as one-sided as they feel at the moment. She touches my cheeks and nose, and then my lips. She leans in.

For a brief flash, I think she wants to breathe in my scent, the way I sometimes breathe hers in when we sleep.

But then her mouth is on mine, and I realize that this is something very different. Her lips press urgently against me, and then I am shocked to feel her tongue slick against the seam of my mouth. A bolt of lust rocks through me and I clench my fists against my legs, determined not to grab her and somehow ruin this moment.

This is kissing. This is what I catch Fran and Kivian doing all the time. This is what Cat does to Tarekh that turns him into a foolishly grinning idiot. Humans do not have the same hygiene laws we do, and they think nothing of pressing mouth against mouth, of letting tongues dance together as if they are mating. And Iris is kissing me. Her mouth is hungry on mine, and when I part my lips at the touch of her tongue again, she makes a soft sound in her throat and deepens the kiss.

It is like nothing I have felt before. Both intimate and sweet, I can feel every movement of her body, can feel that her tongue is slick and smooth and without a single ridge like a mesakkah tongue has. It rubs up against the length of mine, and then Iris gives a little moan. I'm stunned at how good this feels...and how she is finally, finally welcoming me with her body and caresses.

I kiss her back, trying to rub my tongue against hers like she does to me. It feels awkward, but she does not complain about my lack of expertise. Her arms go around my neck and she makes another soft moan when I tease the tip of my tongue along the part of her lips.

"Make me forget," she whispers. "Remind me that I'm in a good place."

"You're with me," I tell her between presses of my mouth to hers. I am hungry for more, so much more. I love the feel of her slight body pressing against mine as we kiss, and my cock aches, my needs long suppressed. "In my bed. In my arms."

"Take my virginity," she whispers, rubbing up against my chest. "Make it so no one wants to buy me ever again."

19

ALYVOS

*H*er strange words make me pause. Of all the sexy, enticing things I imagine her saying...those are not anywhere on the list. I pull back. "What?"

"Kiss me," Iris says, leaning in.

"That's not what you said." I gently pull back from her, studying her lovely face. I don't even care about the scars—they don't mar the beauty of her features. "What do you mean, make it so no one buys you?"

"I...nothing." The grip she has on my shoulders becomes desperate. "Please, let's just leave it be."

This isn't like her, though. Iris never mentions being a slave. It's like it's easier for her to compartmentalize that part of her life and move past it. So for her to bring it up means that something has pushed it into the forefront of her mind. "Was this what your nightmares were about? What brought them on?"

Her hands clench in my tunic. "Just promise me that I'm safe here."

I can feel her trembling. "Of course you're safe."

She nods and holds herself stiffly for a moment before letting her shoulders slump. For a moment she looks exhausted and fragile, and I wonder again what brought this on. "It's just a bad dream," I tell her, stroking a hand down her arm. "I'm here and I won't let anyone touch you."

"Thank you," she says, hiding behind her politeness again. But she lies back down in the bed and pulls the covers tight against her body.

I reach out and caress her cheek, and she grabs my hand and presses her mouth to my knuckles. "I'm sorry about kissing you."

"Why are you sorry? I liked it."

"I just don't want things to change between us." Iris's low whisper sounds full of fear. "I don't think I like change. Not anymore."

I can't deny that I don't want things to change between us—I want more from her than just friendship—but now is not the time to push, especially when she's so fragile. I'm worried, though. This flash of vulnerability isn't like her. Not when she's used to hiding everything behind a polite smile. I want to haul her into my arms and stroke her hair until this fear of hers eases, but I'm not sure she'd welcome my touch. Even now, despite that fierce kiss, she's pulling away.

I pull the blankets against her shoulders and tuck them along her body. "Let me undress and I'll join you in bed."

She nods and I strip my clothes off, distracted by concerned thoughts of the human so close by. I've never thought of Iris as truly fragile until tonight. Mentally strong, yes. Delicate but with a steel core. Damaged but made stronger for it. Tonight, she doesn't seem like any of those things. She seems smaller, terrified, and it pulls at my heart.

I want to help my mate, but she won't let me...and she doesn't even know she's my mate. I think of the way she offered herself to me, and it leaves a sour taste in my mouth. Not just because of the words she used—make it so no one ever buys me again—but because I was tempted.

Lost in my own thoughts, it takes me a moment to realize she's addressing me when she speaks. "Do you ever let strangers on the *Fool*?"

"Strangers?"

"Like...customers. People that you work with for jobs." Her body is tense.

"Rarely. This is our home and we prefer no one invade it unless we want them there." I shrug off my tunic and toss it into a nearby chair, then pull off my belt and kick off my boots. "Besides, we don't trust our clients enough to invite them into our home. We do our business in cantinas."

"So no one would find me if I never left the ship?"

Is that what this is about? Who does she think is going to find her? I sit down on the bed next to her and gently reach out to touch her shoulder. "Iris, who do you think is looking for you?" When she doesn't answer, my frustration and concern grow. "I can't help you if you can't trust me, love."

Her expression is utterly calm for a long moment, so long I think she's not going to answer me. Then, she lets out a long, shuddering sigh and reaches for me. I touch her fingers with mine and when she grips onto my hand tightly, I realize she's trembling. Hard. "I was listening to the bands while you were gone and I heard his name." Her voice is a mere whisper, as if even speaking of this terrifies her.

"Who?" She just needs to say his name and I'll keffing kill him, whoever it is. Anyone that inspires this much terror in my female is not going to draw breath much longer.

"Lord Unto." The name means nothing to me until she shudders and continues. "He's the one that was going to buy me. The one that had me blinded."

Then I know, and my heart fills with rage.

20

IRIS

*a*fter I confess everything to Alvos, I still don't feel better.

He holds me close, but I can feel that he's not at ease and neither am I. I can't open my eyes and let the reality of where I am reassure me. I'm in the darkness, and no matter how tightly he holds me against his chest, I still think about Lord Unto every time I go to sleep. His long, horrible name and his cruel, cruel heart. I've never met the man and I know he's pure evil. I don't need to meet him to know. I can't imagine a person that would blind a horse or a dog that wasn't behaving. I know that a lot of these aliens view humans as little more than animals or pets, but who would do that to a pet? Only the worst kind of person.

The fact that he's out there haunts me. For a few weeks, I've been able to pretend like I'm safe, that everything is all right. But this Lord Unto could claim his property at any time. What do I do then?

I made Alvos promise that he wouldn't tell the others that I'd heard Lord Unto's name. That it'd be a secret just between us, because I want to avoid him and any sort of confrontation possible. I just want to hide away from Unto's corner of the universe and pray that he never finds me.

After all, I'm sure escaping is considered very, very bad behavior, and I can only imagine what body parts he'll remove if he has me in his possession again. The thought haunts me and I huddle against Alvos's chest all night. I sleep very little and when I do, my dreams are of captivity.

I wake up the next morning feeling less rested than ever, and it's hard to leave my room. Part of me wants to hide away forever, but I know that'll just make the others wonder what's going on, and so it's easier to pretend that everything's normal. I force myself out of bed, dress, and then head for the mess hall. I can hear people moving around in the room, though it's quiet when I enter. There's a lightly rolling hum under my feet that tells me that the ship's moving. We've left the station, and I can't say I'm sorry to realize that. The farther away we are from this place, the better.

"Morning," I call out in a greeting to the others, forcing a smile to my face. I put a hand out, touching the edge of one of the tables to guide me. "Is there any tea on?"

"Iris. Good. You're here." Kivian's voice is crisp and business-like without any of its usual good humor, and I feel a prickle of alarm.

"I am," I answer calmly. "Who all is in here with us?"

"Everyone," Alvos says, speaking up, and I'm torn between a ripple of pleasure at the sound of his buttery, rich voice, and fear, because everyone in here at the same time never happens. Something is up.

I force myself to remain calm. "Oh?" I turn toward his voice—he's seated at the table I'm standing next to. The air feels still near me, and I reach out to see if the seat is empty. It is, so I slide into it. "What's going on?"

"We're just discussing our next job." Fran sounds quiet, subdued.

"Oh?" A hand brushes mine. I recognize the callused fingers and the fuzzy-soft skin—Alvos. He wants to hold my hand. I don't know if I'm pleased or worried. It feels like something is wrong. I twine my fingers through his and force my voice to be placid and even. "What's the next job? I thought we were hooking someone at the station with gambling."

"That can happen anytime," Kivian says. "This particular job is more time sensitive. We're intercepting a shipment."

"What kind of shipment?" I ask idly, since it's awfully quiet in the room. If everyone's in here, they're not talking.

Someone clears a throat. Male. I don't know who.

Then, Alvos squeezes my hand. "You know who we're going after."

Cold washes over me. This is why everyone is here, then. This is why it's quiet and feels fraught with tension in the room. "You're going after Lord Unto," I comment, my voice mild and bland as could be. Inside, I'm screaming. Outwardly, though, I'm so very calm.

"Full name is Lord Unto'Abarri'Nil Vohs Bekhinto, Lord of Nine Sunrises and Ruler of the Thirteenth Moon," says Kivian, and then he snorts. "Pompous ass." No one laughs despite his pause, so he continues. "He's getting a shipment of illegal goods. Likely some human slaves, possibly other forbidden species. We don't think it's darkmatter or weaponry shipments because he's got a very small crew with him. We've touched base with a few contacts and found out that he's currently vacationing on his barge near Ekhos II's water moon. It's a good time to slide over, hijack his vessel, lift his newly bought friends, and send his ship into the sun. It's going to be quite the unfortunate accident."

"I can't keffing wait," Alvos growls.

"It'll be dangerous," Fran warns. "He's likely got a complete crew with him. That means guards and security out the wazoo."

"I like dangerous," my Alvos says, and cracks his knuckles. "Just let me have a chance."

"There's no denying this lord needs to be taken down a notch," Kivian says. "I'm just not sure we've got the manpower to be the ones to do it."

I desperately hope someone will speak up. Someone will be reasonable and say no, it's too much to handle. That there will be other jobs.

"Of course we do," Alvos says, and he sounds eager for a fight. My broken, bloodthirsty Alvos. "This guy's not touching my Iris ever again. We take him down."

"If everyone's in agreement," Kivian says. "Iris?"

"I'm not crew. Not really. I can't decide for you," I say, and I'm so very calm. Alvos squeezes my hand, but I don't squeeze back. It doesn't matter that I asked him not to say anything. He told the others and now we're going after Lord Unto. It's my worst nightmare come to life. They know it's dangerous. They just don't care enough.

"What about *The Obsidian Blade*?" Cat asks. "Tarekh says he heard a rumor that they tried to board him a few months back and got creamed. Space particles everywhere."

I go cold.

Alvos only laughs and squeezes my hand. "Their crew was useless. The *Blade* couldn't board a ship piloted by kits. I don't know how they thought they could take on a fully manned barge. We're smarter than that."

The others murmur agreement, but I don't listen. All I can think about is Lord Unto. Someone that brutal is sure to be surrounded by guards. I've been told Alvos and the others are good fighters, but I don't know them well enough to be reassured that all will be fine. Instead, I try to imagine what will happen if they try to board the ship and fail. I'll be enslaved again. Fran and Cat, too. The others will be killed.

Alvos will be killed.

A hard lump forms in my throat and I think of the man at my side. Of touching his face late at night and feeling his smile. His fuzzy skin taut over hard muscles, and the way his chest feels when a laugh rumbles out of him.

How gentle and caring he is with me.

If I lose him, I'm going to be broken beyond repair. I know I'm already damaged and struggling, but he's the one thing that's keeping me together. I can't lose him.

I remain silent while the others discuss plans and strategy. There's a way to disable the barge without getting on their radar, it seems. One person can take an escape pod toward the other ship, which won't pull up on their scanners. Once the pod gets close enough, the pilot can suit up and drift out to the other ship in space. He'll attach a sensor that will make the ship think that there's a problem with the engine, and while it sends out false signals, the *Fool* will swoop in and attach. Alvos and Tarekh and Kivian are going to board immediately with Cat and Fran providing backup. They've done it all a dozen times before, apparently, and from the sounds of their voices, it's a routine job for them.

Alvos is going to be on the escape pod. He's going to be the one drifting in space in nothing but a suit, attaching the sensor to the underside of the barge. If they find him, they'll kill him immediately. Just the thought makes my entire body clench up with worry, though Alvos's hand is loose in mine as if it's no problem. No big deal.

It's a big deal to me, though.

I don't say anything aloud, of course. I just listen. I'll remain on the bridge with Sentorr and listen to comms to make sure no one's coming in with the authorities or bringing reinforcements. It's all figured out.

I hear chairs scrape back and the sound of people getting to their feet. "If no one has anything else to bring up, I'll set the ship to surging," Sentorr says. When no one speaks up, he continues. "Very well, then. Surging in five minutes. Remember to strap yourselves in."

There's a low murmur of chatter as people leave the room. I remain seated, and Alvos squeezes my hand. When it calms and feels like we're alone, he speaks. "You're quiet."

I pull my hand from his. "I'm fine."

I'm not fine. I'm terrified and angry both. He told them about Lord Unto even after I begged him not to, and now they're all going to risk their lives to rob him. They can say it's because of money or slaves or whatever, but it's because I spoke up. I know it is. And Alvos is taking on the most dangerous role of them all. I try to picture him drifting silently out in space to sneak up on the barge, and I'm terrified.

What if I lose him? I've worked so hard over the last few weeks to become more independent, and yet the thought of losing Alvos steals the breath from my lungs. It's not that I need him to guide me through the ship or be my friend.

It's that I need him. I need his presence. I need his affection and support. I need more than just that brief kiss from last night.

Have I fallen in love without even realizing it? Because being in his arms feels like the most natural thing in the world suddenly, and now I'm wondering if I'm going to lose that. I feel like I'm dying inside. The despair shooting through me feels like I'm losing my sight all over again, except this time I'm going to lose my heart.

I can't handle this. I get to my feet and head out of the room.

I hear Alvos, just a few steps behind me. He doesn't speak until I turn towards the bedroom. "You should go to the bridge," he says. "Belt in. We're going to lose gravity when we surge, and I don't want you getting hurt."

HE doesn't want ME getting hurt. I want to laugh (or scream), but all I do is continue forward, keeping my expression safely pleasant. "I'll be careful."

Alvos makes a frustrated sound and I wait to hear his boots heading away, but he follows me back to our quarters. Of course he does. He's protective and sweet and if he thinks there's even a whiff of danger when it comes to me, he's going to do his best to make sure I'm all right. Just like with this stupid barge attack.

It won't matter to him if it costs him his life. And that's the part that makes me angriest. The bitter frustration and helplessness seethe through me with every step. By the time I touch the door and then run my hand over the sensor panel to let myself in, I'm fuming with pent-up rage.

He follows right behind me. Of course he does. Once the door slides shut with its little whirr that tells me we're alone, Alvos grabs my arm and spins me around to face him. "Why won't you talk to me?" His voice is blunt with irritation.

"There's nothing to say." I keep my voice mild and sweet. "Nothing's wrong."

Alvos makes another frustrated sound in his throat. "Then why are you coming back here to hide in our quarters instead of going on the bridge?"

Because I don't want to, I'm tempted to bite out. My expression is calm. So, so calm. "What makes you think that there's a problem?"

He growls low in his throat. "Because I know you, Iris. I know how your mind works and you retreat behind this nicey-nice shit whenever you're scared. You don't show me what you're feeling because you're afraid to for some reason, and that makes me crazy. Is this how it's going to be between us?"

"Is what how it's going to be between us?" I ask mildly. He's not wrong about any of that, and I can't decide if it makes me upset or scares me.

"Don't do this," he snarls, and I feel his hands on my shoulders. "Don't you hide what you're thinking from me. Show me something, damn it! Anything! You're not a keffing automaton. I know you've got emotion under there! Quit hiding it from me!"

My anger and fear for him bubbles over. I reach out and punch him.

Or at least, I try to. I always forget how tall he is, and my hand ends up skimming along his jaw, but the meaning is there.

It's utterly silent in the room.

A wave of fear washes over me and I sag, my knees giving out. *No, no, no,* my brain is screaming. *Now you're not safe.* I want to collapse on the ground in a heap of apologies and obedience.

But Alvos won't let me. He laughs, and the sound is delighted even as he sweeps me into his arms and off of my feet. "Oh no you don't," he murmurs. "That's the first real emotion you've shown me other than last night. Don't be scared. Tell me what you're thinking, because I keffing love it. Slap me again if you want to." There's a timbre in his voice I've never heard before, as if he's aroused.

I suck in a breath, because I can't decide if I'm aroused at his response or just really, really mad. I slap at his chest even as he cradles me against him. "Does it matter what I'm thinking?" Slap. Slap. "It's all been decided already."

"It has," he agrees.

Now he's the calm one, and it infuriates me. I slap his chest again. "I told you about my fears in private. *In private.* And you went and told the others right away. You promised you wouldn't!"

"I'm not going to let him get away with this," Alvos says, as if it's all a done deal. So I smack him again with my open palm, because the bastard's not sorry in the least. "I'm sorry, Iris, but your safety comes first to me. He's going to pay for hurting you, and then I'm going to make sure he never hurts anyone else again."

"I. Don't. Care. About. That!" With each word, I smack his shoulder again. It feels good, and I can't stop myself. I close my hand into a fist and lightly punch him. My blows are ineffectual against his armored skin, but it's not about the pain, it's about getting this all out of my system. "You're going to get killed!"

"I won't."

His smug, confident answer just infuriates me more. "I'm so...*mad* at you right now. Put me down!"

"I like you mad." He's utterly unruffled. "And it doesn't matter how angry you get—I'm not changing my mind."

"Then let someone else go in the pod! Let someone else risk their necks. Stay here on the ship with me!" I clench my hands in his tunic because I want to throttle the man. I don't know how to get rid of all of this frustrated energy, so I just hold fistfuls of his shirt and shake angrily. "Don't do this to prove a point!"

"It's not to prove a point," Alvos says. "It's because I love you and you're mine."

I suck in a breath. For a moment I want to punch him in the face and kiss him both. The urge to kiss wins, though, and I unclench one handful of tunic and find his jaw, and then lean in, hoping he'll meet me halfway.

He gives a little groan and then his lips brush over mine in a light caress. I want more than a gentle kiss, though. I'm too fired up, and everything's exploding out of me. I tighten my hand on his tunic and push my mouth against his harder, practically savage in my movements. I'm hungry with need as I move my tongue against the seam of his lips, insisting on entry. I want to give him a kiss that will show him just how frustrated and full of emotion I am. He wants me to show him something? I'll show him everything. So I kiss him hard, bruising my lips as our teeth come together. It's not polite or sweet, but fierce and angry and vicious.

And good. So, so good.

21

IRIS

*H*is tongue rubs against mine as the kiss deepens, and I remember the strangely arousing ridges he has on it and how they feel when they drag against my tongue. I moan against his lips as he sweeps into my mouth, and then I fight with him for control of the kiss, and it turns into a battle of its own, both of us vying for dominance. Faster and harder we kiss until I'm breathless with lust and my mouth is throbbing and our teeth clash as we kiss and still it's not enough.

Somewhere outside the room, there's a low whine and then the entire ship surges forward. Our bodies rock and Alvos staggers backward a step, and then I begin to lift out of his arms.

There's no more gravity. We're surging.

I gasp and hold on to him, locking my hand tight in the soft fabric of his tunic. He's floating, I think, and my hair streams around my face. Something flutters against my cheek—the end of my ribbon,

I think—and then it's a bit like swimming without the weight of water around us. There's no anchor as I drift upward.

His hand touches my cheek, rough and reassuring. "I've got you, love. I won't let go." Something hitches onto the belt of my jumper—his other hand—and then I'm anchored against him. "Don't be scared."

"I'm not scared," I whisper, shoving my streaming, wild hair away from my face. It's dangerously close to getting into my mouth. "You've got me, right?" And for some reason, that sounds incredibly sexy. I'm getting aroused. Maybe it's the situation or the hint of danger or the kiss we just shared, but I can feel the heat throbbing between my legs and I like it. I want more kisses. I want to run my hands all over him. I want more of everything—and not just because I don't want to be a virgin anymore.

It's because I truly want Alvos. No, his name is Alyvos, I tell myself. I have to stop hiding, to stop pushing to see if he'll respond negatively. I know in my heart he won't. I know he's mine and I'm safe with him. "Alyvos," I say softly, letting it roll off my tongue. "I love you."

The big alien groans again, and I feel him drift closer to me as he tugs on my belt, hauling our bodies together. "My sweet Iris. Will you trust me? Don't be scared of this Lord whoever. I won't let him harm another hair on your head. You're my female. No one's going to touch you ever again."

His breath fans hot on my cheek, and I feel a shiver ripple through my body. My nipples rub against the front of my jumper and I feel hot and achy all over. "Are we still drifting?" I ask in a soft voice as I lean in. The short strands of his hair tickle against my skin as I do.

"Yes. We will until we stop surging. It's dangerous if you're not tied down when you stop, because you can get dumped pretty hard. That's why people belt in."

"But until then, we're safe?" I extend one leg and feel his thigh brush against my leg, and I automatically hook it around him. Then, I'm straddling his thigh and that sends new shockwaves of feeling through me.

Alyvos groans and cups the back of my head. He buries his face against my neck and I can feel his horn rub against the side of my face, all warm metal and hard surface. His tongue slicks against my collarbone and sends a jolt right to my pussy. "You're always safe, love. I'd never let you get hurt."

I drag my fingers through his drifting hair. "Kiss me again," I demand, and he makes a sound that's a cross between a huff of amusement and pleasure.

"Are you scared?" he demands back.

"No." I rub up and down against his thigh, determined to show him just now unafraid I am. Of course, that small movement increases the friction of his body against mine and I'm so turned on that I gasp. I never thought that humping on someone's leg could be so damn sexy, but it's making me crazy with need. "I'm not scared of anything you do."

"I never thought it'd be so sexy when a female hit me," he murmurs, and then I feel his breath against my ear. A second later, his teeth scrape over the skin and I instinctively rub against his thigh again. "You gonna smack me around a few more times, fierce little thing?"

Shuddering, I lean in, and when my face brushes against his, I bite at his jaw. I love the tremor that moves through him, the soft intake of his breath that tells me he likes that as much as I do.

And because I'm feeling bold and powerful, I tug at his collar. "Show me how this comes off."

For a moment, I expect him to refuse me. To point out that I propositioned him for sex last night because I was panicky and feeling helpless. But this is different in every way, and he only chuckles and touches something at his neck, and in the next moment, the fabric of the tunic is loose under my grip.

Greedy with eagerness, I push the material aside and slide my hands over his bare chest. I've touched him furtively while we were in the bed together, but it was always a slightly different sort of vibe between us. Those were accidental brushes of skin against skin, or innocent explorations of his shape to learn his appearance. Today, my touch isn't innocent at all and I moan when my fingertips catch against the hard edge of the thick plate over his breastbone. It's fascinating and alien and sexy all at once. "What color is this?"

"Blue, just like everything else. Just darker blue."

"Mmm." I mentally picture it and love the visual in my head. "You're not as soft here." I let my fingers play over his chest.

Alyvos groans. "Never tell a male he's soft."

"But you are. You're so soft to the touch here." I let my fingers slide under one plate's edges, caressing the skin there. "And here." I trace a finger along his collarbone. "It's fascinating to touch you. I feel like there's always more to explore and learn."

"And you're not scared? Of the fact that I'm an alien?"

I shake my head. Maybe I was once, but he's proven to me over and over again that he's nothing like the ones that captured me. He's different in every way, and I trust him. So I pull his tunic open wider and float in to kiss at his thick neck. "Does it bother you that I'm human?"

"Never." He pauses and then his hand skims down my back, caressing my spine. "You ready for this between us, love? I'm not sure you're thinking clearly—"

"Don't tell me what I think." I slap at his chest again and then rake my nails over the plates of his chest and feel him shudder against me.

Alyvos groans again. "Kef me, love, but it's incredible when you're fierce like this."

Does he truly think so? Because it's making me wild. I'm a little surprised that letting go like this feels so good. I put a hand to his jaw to find his mouth and lean in to give him another hard, fierce kiss. I bite at his lip. I claw at his chest. All of it just gets me hotter, and judging from the noises he makes, he feels the same way. His tail flicks against my butt, as if it wants in on the action, too, and I even like how it feels. I like everything.

And I'm excited to experience more. I nip at his lip again, loving that I feel sharp fangs when I run my tongue over his teeth. "Can I finish undressing you?"

"I'd be sad if you didn't." His hands are on my belt, holding me so I don't float away. "I'm yours to do whatever you want with."

I like that thought most of all. I let one hand go to his chest again, and then pull at his tunic. I imagine that it's open in a big sexy vee that shows off his blue abs, and I feel a twinge of sadness that I don't get to see what must be a visual delight for myself. But my remaining senses are heightened, and I tell myself that I notice things that I wouldn't before, like the delicious scent of his body, which is musky and appealing, or his skin, which fascinates me endlessly with its texture.

And then it doesn't matter, because I'm letting my fingers glide down his hard, muscled abdomen and I don't need eyes to know how incredible his body is. His chest is so hard it's like caressing warm marble. I graze over the divot of his navel and then skim lower. "I just realized you're completely hairless except for your head. Do you have body hair...elsewhere?" Am I blushing? I bet I'm blushing. It's a weird thing to ask, but I want to visualize his appearance.

"No. Does that bother you?"

"I do. Does that bother you?"

He makes a husky little growl in his throat. "Never. I think that little patch of hair between your thighs is sexy."

I bite my lip and wriggle on his thigh. He's so big and hard between my legs that I'm tempted to stop my exploration of him and just grind out a quick, brutal orgasm against that massive leg. God, that would just be so naughty and wrong...and I love the thought of it.

But then I'd have to stop touching Alyvos, and that's the last thing I want to do. I'm just now getting to the good stuff. There'll be time enough for grinding later. I move my hands to his belt and then tug the loose material of his long tunic free. "If you take this off, what are you still wearing?" I'm so breathless I don't even recognize my own voice. "Describe it to me."

"Trou. Just plain gray trou. I don't dress fancy like Kivian." Something tugs on a floating lock of my hair and I realize he's caressing it. "And boots."

I slide a hand down his hip and over his thigh. "You're so big and muscular. I'm trying to picture all of you in my head." In my mind he's mouthwateringly gorgeous. The body under my hands sure is.

"Take all the time you need to see me," Alyvos murmurs, and his hand skims over my shoulder, caressing me. I love that small touch and want to lean into it, but the slightest movement makes us float and bump away.

I make a sound of frustration as we drift apart again, and he hitches a hand in my belt once more.

"We can always wait for gravity to return," Alyvos tells me, a huff of amusement in his voice.

"No," I tell him, and wrap my arms around his torso—or try to. He's big and brawny and I'm pretty sure I look like a barnacle against him, but I don't care. I hold on tight and press my mouth to his skin. "I've slept against you for far too many unfulfilled nights already. I want you and I'm tired of waiting."

He groans and his hand drags down my back, then cups my butt cheek. "You could have reached for me on any of those nights, you know. I would have been more than happy to pleasure you even if you weren't ready for a full mating."

I shudder, my mind filling with visuals of him "pleasuring" me. "I wasn't sure until I kissed you if you felt the same way—"

Alyvos takes the hand I have on his chest and drags it downward. A moment later my palm is pressed against something thick and hot and very, very big. "Do you feel that, Iris? I've been hard for the last week and a half waiting for you to touch me. I've wanted you since the moment I saw you. I knew you were mine the moment you reached for me."

Fascinated, I stroke the length of him, learning him with my hand. The fabric of his trou is strange, kind of a cross between plastic and cotton, and rustles when I caress him. I can feel the outline of him through the material, and I pause, because in addition to how mouthwateringly thick he is, I feel...ridges. And that can't be right. But when I stroke over him again and hear the hiss of his breath, I realize that I'm not wrong. He's got thick, hard ridges along the length of his cock reminiscent of his tongue.

Oh...my.

"Your hand feels incredible." There's a husky rawness in his voice that makes my pussy clench in response. I love the grit in his tone, as if he's barely holding on to control. And when I slide my hand up and down his length, I love the twitch of response his body gives. It's like he can't help himself and has to move against me.

I know how that feels. "Kiss me again?" I whisper, because I want his mouth on me.

With a hungry groan, one big hand cups the back of my head and then his mouth is on mine and I'm being kissed as if nothing else in the world exists but our two mouths. I whimper at how good it feels and stroke his cock through his pants again, wanting him to buck up against my grip once more. I want him to lose control at my touch. He rocks into my hand once, twice, and then breaks the kiss with an explosion of breath. "You're going to make me come too quickly, love," he tells me.

"Is that a bad thing?"

Laughter rumbles through his chest, making me shiver. "Only because it ends the fun far too quickly. Come here." He hooks a strong arm around my waist, and then I feel a surge as he pushes off of the wall. A moment later, we bounce onto the softness of the bed and then I feel a gentle little tug as he pulls me back down again. Alyvos guides my hand to the headboard, where there's a metal bar going lengthwise across. "Hold on to this."

I do, sliding both hands around the metal and waiting. My hips immediately begin to rise, because there's no gravity to hold me down against the mattress.

Something soft curls around my ankle—Alyvos's tail. It holds me down and I feel one of his hands rest on my belly. "I'm going to undress you," he tells me in a heated voice. "I want to kiss every inch of your body. Especially that little dark tuft of hair between your thighs."

I moan, imagining his big head between my legs. I fooled around with a few dates back on Earth, but I never got quite that far. The thought of the man I love putting his mouth there makes me shudder, and I can feel just how slick my pussy's getting when I shift on the bed.

"I can smell just how wet you are," he rasps, and then nuzzles the vee of my thighs.

I gasp, because I swear I can feel his mouth through the fabric, and I'm shocked at just how strong a surge of arousal washes through me. I've never felt so turned on, like I'm going to die if he doesn't do that again right away. I grip the bar on the bed, holding my breath as I wait for his next touch. Being blind makes the anticipation that much greater, I realize, because I can't see what my lover's about to do. "What are you going to do?" I ask.

"I'm going to unwrap this pussy," he tells me, and a hot hand skims over my lower belly. "And then I'm going to taste it."

As I lie there on the bed, I quiver in anticipation, waiting for his next touch. I expect it anywhere—leg, hips, breasts, doesn't matter to me. I welcome any touch. But when I feel the ribbon slither off of my brow, I'm stunned.

Alyvos pulls it off and then brushes a knuckle over my temple. "You're beautiful."

I swallow hard, because there's an emotional knot in my throat I can't quite shake. "I'm messed up." I don't need eyes to feel the horrible scars. I touch them every morning and I can feel the upraised ridges where they healed badly.

"Not to me. Nothing anyone else did to you changes how lovely I find you. You're perfect to me." Before I can tell him that he's wrong, his thumb moves over my mouth, and then he slides his hand downward, between my breasts. "And I need you naked."

I know he's distracting me, but that's all right. I don't want this to turn into an argument about how I can't be pretty without eyes. I want him to keep touching me. And when his hand moves over the fastener of my jumper and the material loosens, I hold my breath with anticipation of his next touch.

A whimper explodes out of me when his hand grazes over my bared breast. "So lovely," Alyvos murmurs. "You're built differently than mesakkah women. They're not rounded here. I think I prefer this."

I nearly come off the bed when his thumb rubs over my nipple. I cry out and I hear his breath quicken in response. He jerks at my belt, as if suddenly as desperate as me. In the next moment, I feel his hand ripping at my clothing even as something hot and wet latches over my breast.

His mouth.

Oh god.

My body rocks upward against the bed and I strain against his mouth. We bump and shift in the gravity-free environment, and I cling to the bar to keep me pinned—sort of—to the bed. I'm floating up, but it doesn't matter, because he presses a hand against my belly and pushes me back down on the bed, and then his mouth is on my nipple again, teasing and licking. I feel each stroke of his tongue and it sends a pulse between my thighs. I'm moaning and squirming by the time he moves to the other breast, and I barely pay attention when the rest of my clothing falls backward onto the bed in a heap, the fasteners completely undone.

I'm naked under him.

Alyvos's tongue glides between my breasts and his hand pushes on my hips, keeping me against the mattress. My hands are sweating with nervousness as I hold on to the metal bar on the headboard, but I don't think the big alien cares. He's licking a path down my belly and making soft noises of approval in his throat as he tastes me. "Perfect," he breathes, and then one big hand cups my pussy, covering it.

Just that simple touch makes me squirm with need.

"Look at how wet you are," he breathes. "So juicy and sweet, waiting for my mouth. You like the thought of that, don't you?" His thumb plays across the curls of my pussy, teasing me without ever delving deeper.

"Touch me," I beg, unable to stand it.

"I am touching you," Alyvos tells me, and he slides his thumb along the seam of my pussy. "Is there any particular way you want it?"

I'm sucking in deep breaths, squirming. I should tell him exactly where I want his mouth and fingers, but it feels so bold and all of my boldness—my slapping, feisty boldness from earlier—is deserting me. Truthfully, I wouldn't mind if he put his mouth back on my breasts again. They're aching with the need for his touch. But...that would be like settling for cake instead of ice cream when you've been promised ice cream. It'll be good...but it's still not ice cream.

I've been passive for so long, though, that the words die in my throat. I don't know how to ask, or even if I can. I just pant and wait for him to touch me, hoping silently that he'll realize my struggle.

He pets me for a moment more, and then his other hand slides up my thigh. "Maybe I should just explore you and find out for myself, hmm?"

The pent-up breath explodes from my lungs. "Please," I whisper.

"Of course, love." He sounds so confident, so assured. Like he's got me. Like I can relax. Like I'm not going to fall apart if I say the wrong thing. He pets the curls of my pussy one more time and then strokes a finger deeper, exploring me. The wet sound my flesh makes is utterly filthy in the quiet room and is quickly followed by his bass rumble of pleasure. "You're coating my fingers, love. I can't stop looking at how turned on you are. How ready for me." He pushes my folds apart and then places one hand over the lower part of my belly, pinning me against the bed as I float up once more. "Mmm, look at that."

I squirm. I can't help it. I'm splayed open for his attentions and it's making me crazy. "What is it?"

"You've got a little nub here," Alyvos murmurs, and then his finger traces a circle around my clit.

Ecstasy shoots through me. I cry out in startled pleasure, my body clenching in response. Nothing's ever felt as good as that one little touch, and I can feel my cheeks heat with embarrassment at his low chuckle.

"I think I've figured out where you'd like to be touched," my big alien murmurs. "What's this called?"

"It's a clit," I whisper.

"And it feels good?"

"Oh, yeah." I practically moan my response because his finger is dipping through the slickness of my folds again, teasing closer without actually touching it. I'm barely aware of how wide my legs are spread on the bed, or that I'm silently rocking my hips in a little undulation, my entire body begging for his next touch. All I know is that I'm going to go crazy if he doesn't do it soon. "Alyvos, please," I beg.

"Mmm, I like the way you say my name, pretty one." I feel a hot nip and realize he's nibbling on the inside of my knee. "Say it again, just like that."

"Alyvos," I breathe obediently, saying it perfectly. No more games. No more testing the waters. I trust him.

I love him.

22

IRIS

"My sweet Iris," Alyvos says, and nuzzles the inside of my thigh. I squirm again, but it's not enough. It's never enough. I need his mouth—or his fingers, I'm not picky —back to my clit. I need him to touch me and show me that sensation again. I feel hollow and achy deep between my thighs, as if I'm missing something I've never had. It's the strangest feeling.

Of course, a moment later he rubs one slick fingertip against my clit again, and I forget all about everything but that touch. The air gusts out of my lungs and I'm a moaning, delirious mess as he explores me, teasing and learning my clit and the best ways to touch it. Little light circles seem to be the best, though I love every touch he gives me. It's the circles that make me arch, trying to press harder against his fingers, so full of need I can't stand it. I feel as if I'm going to come out of my own skin. I don't care about the sounds I'm making in my throat—or the sounds my body is making as his fingers glide through my wet folds. I'm addicted to his touch already. Nothing matters but the feel of his fingers teasing my flesh.

Then, I feel his mouth descend, hot and demanding. There's a subtle lick against my folds, and then I hear him groan low. "Kef me, you taste good, Iris. So good. I'm going to lick this pussy for days." His mouth is on me again a moment later, and his tongue repeats the movements of his fingers from just a short time ago— little circling licks flicking against my sensitive clit, determined to drive me over the edge and make me crazy with need.

It's too much. I lose my grip on the headboard and reach down for his head, desperate to grab on to something. I find his big, curling horns and hold tight as he licks and nuzzles my pussy right toward the hardest orgasm of my entire life.

I come so hard that my entire body clenches tight and I nearly black out from the sheer pleasure of it.

He continues to lick my pussy with that crazily erotic ridged tongue of his. My entire body feels sensitized and I'm whimpering every time he drags the tip over my folds. "You taste so good, love. I've never tasted anything better."

"Alyvos," I breathe, over and over again. His name comes to my lips with every stroke of his tongue, and even though I just climaxed, I feel ready practically all over again. "Please. I need you."

Finally, my alien lifts his head from my pussy and presses a kiss to my thigh. "You want me to wear plas-film? I can get up and get some."

"What is that?" Dazed, I try to picture what he's talking about. "Condoms?"

"It's a film that covers your skin," he tells me, continuing to press his mouth to my thigh as if addicted. "So I can't transfer diseases or my seed into your body."

"So it is like a condom." When I feel his body move, I realize he's shrugging. "Are you diseased, then?"

"No."

"Can you get me pregnant?"

"Not without medical assistance, I'm afraid." His tongue flicks against my skin.

"Then stay with me." I stroke a hand down his horns, then caress his cheek. "Forget about that and just stay with me. We'll do this skin to skin."

Alyvos groans. "Keffing love when you say such sexy things."

I can't help but chuckle. "Is that sexy then?"

"Honestly, everything you say is sexy." I hear a rustle of fabric and his body shifts against mine. He's undressing the rest of the way. His tail clenches tight along my leg and then moves away. A second later, his weight shifts over me once more, and I feel nothing but glorious, wonderful skin.

I sigh with contentment as his body settles over mine. "You feel so good."

His hand skims over the length of my back and I realize belatedly that we're floating once more. Oh. At some point I let go of the bed and we're both midair. I slide my arms around him, and when his mouth brushes over mine, I let out a moan because it feels so good.

Alyvos's strong arms hitch one of my thighs around his hips, and I automatically move the other so I'm clasping him tight between my legs. I can feel my hair drifting into my face and my body feels light and airy, and I'm surrounded by the heat of his bigger form. It's fascinating and sexy all at once, and I love when his mouth captures mine once more, as if he can't stand to have us apart in any way at all.

I slide my hand down his stomach, eager to feel him...and run into something strange. Protruding out of his groin is a hard, finger-like appendage, and I flinch away when I run across it. "Um...what's that?"

"A spur?" He nuzzles at my face. "Have you never seen a male naked before, my sweet?"

I bite back the surge of laughter bubbling in my throat, because no man wants to be laughed at when he's naked atop a girl. He just sounds so confident that I'm a blushing, sheltered thing. A virgin, yes. Sheltered, no. "I have. Human men don't have a spur." Though this does explain why Cat and Fran went into hysterics when we were playing Choices. "What's it for?"

His tongue flicks against my earlobe, his breath hot. "Must it be for something? What is your little clit for?"

He's got me there. I'm having a hard time concentrating with his tongue playing along the shell of my ear. "So it...feels good?" I gasp as he rocks the hard length of him against my grip.

"Not as good as your little bud, but good enough." He nips at my ear and thrusts into my hand again. "Spread your thighs wider for me, sweet love."

I do as he asks, and he takes my hand from his cock and moves it to his hip. His mouth captures mine again even as something hard and hot presses against my core. His cock, I realize a scant second before he presses forward.

Tight heat blooms through my body, and it feels as if something very large is being forced into something uncomfortably small. I gasp against his mouth, and he swallows my breath with a kiss. I know that my body will adjust, so I fall into his kiss and let his lips and tongue distract me as I wait for my muscles to relax and allow him in. I knew he would feel big, but I wasn't expecting how taut my own body would feel...or how good the ache of it would be.

His body pushing into mine steals away all thought. I'm lost in the sensation as he kisses me, and Alyvos's first slow, subtle thrust draws me back into my body. I moan against his mouth as he rocks forward, moving a little deeper with slow, steady precision. "Tell me if I hurt you," he murmurs between peppered kisses. I just sigh. It's impossible to tell him that yes, it hurts, but in all the right ways. That the ache is delicious and just makes me hungry for more. That my body's adjusting to his invasion and little shockwaves of pleasure are jolting through me with every twitch of his body.

I don't say any of that. All I do is moan and cling to him.

"My Iris," he rasps, and the sound is so sexy and appealing that it feels as if it ripples through me. "Your cunt is so...keffing...tight."

"Sorry," I whisper, even though I'm not sorry. I just want to hold on to him and feel this forever. I love the sensations moving through us. I've always known sex would be good, but I just never realized how good.

A laugh barks out of him. "Don't you dare apologize." I feel him moving over me, his hips pushing against mine in short little bursts. As he does, something hard rubs up against my clit. His finger? No, I realize a moment later—it's his spur.

And then as he thrusts into me, it drags along the side of my clit, sending pleasure spiraling through my body. Oh god.

That was what Cat and Fran were so nuts about.

I can't stop moaning, and he murmurs soft words to me as he strokes deep. He tells me how beautiful I am, how perfect, how good I feel, how much he loves me. I wish I could pay more attention, but the dual sensations of his cock and his spur teasing me in both spots are making it impossible for me to concentrate. I'm lost in sensation, and when another orgasm rips quickly through me, I'm not surprised at all. And when he speeds up, thrusting faster and harder, I climax again.

And again.

By the time he shudders over me and growls out my name as he comes, I've probably climaxed at least four times. I'm exhausted and wrung out, and I've never felt so damn good. Alyvos collapses on top of me and then presses a kiss to my mouth, and his skin is sweaty and sticky against mine, and that feels good, too.

"Hi," I whisper, loving the feel of his breath tickling my face.

Alyvos nips at my jaw again. "You're incredible."

I chuckle. "Me? All I did was lie here and come. A lot."

His nose rubs against mine, and my heart melts a little. "Give yourself credit. You also screamed as you came a lot."

I smile and hold him closer, and as I do, I realize that even though he's on top of me, I'm not being smothered by his massive size. "Are we still floating?"

"We are. As soon as I can bear to let you go, we should probably strap down so there won't be any accidents." He kisses my jaw again, and then my cheek. "I just can't bear to let you go yet."

I'm okay with that.

23

IRIS

*a*t some point, Alyvos pulls me down against the bed, just in time for gravity to kick in. The ship surges forward and we thump onto the mattress, and everything feels heavy and thick for a while. My legs feel like cement as my alien helps me to the shower and we wash each other off and curl up in bed.

Soon, he's going to be leaving to go after Lord Unto, and I should be mad. I should be anxious and stressed. Instead, I curl up against his warm chest and sleep in his arms, his tail wrapped around my calf. I've never slept better, and it's like my body's betrayed me by letting me sleep so deeply.

I wake up sometime later to the sound of Alyvos pulling on his clothing and the familiar buckle noise his boots make. I know what's going to happen now, and the thought's like lead in my chest.

Even though I don't want him to go, even though I'm terrified that he's going to get killed, my Alyvos is going to board some awful lord's vacation barge and steal from him as if it's no big deal. This might be the last moment I ever spend with him, and the thought makes a knot form in my throat.

I hear him step forward and a moment later, he brushes my messy hair off my brow. "Sleep, love. It'll be a few hours yet before you're needed on the bridge."

Sleep? While he's in danger? Not a chance. Every nerve ending in my body is screaming for him to stay with me. That revenge doesn't matter. That anyone else that Lord Asshole has stolen is on their own. I need him here with me, because if I lose him, I don't know how I'm going to go on. I don't want him to go.

I pull the covers back and expose my body in what's hopefully a sexy pose. "Can I entice you to stay?"

Alyvos groans and a moment later, kisses my forehead. "I wish I could, love."

"No, you don't," I say softly. "You want revenge. You want a fight. What if I told you those things don't matter to me? That having you with me is more than getting even with the guy that ordered me blinded?"

"I can't leave it, Iris," he says. "Don't ask me to."

"Even if it'll change everything between us? If you come back..." Please, please God, let him come back. "I don't know that I can feel the same way knowing you don't respect what I want." It's a harsh gauntlet to throw down, but he has to know how I feel. He has to realize how badly I don't want this. "If you want to hit something more than you want me, then go."

There's a long pause. "It's not like that, Iris."

"Isn't it?" I feel so defeated, so sad. I should be kissing him and enjoying these last few moments with him, and instead, I'm getting angry all over again.

The comm chimes. "You coming up?" Sentorr asks, voice tinny. "Pod's fueled up and ready."

"Be right there."

I pull the blankets over my body and lie back down.

"Iris," he begins.

"Go," I tell him in a dull voice. "There's nothing else to say."

"Isn't there?"

Okay then, he's right. There's one more thing to say. "I thought you loved me, but maybe all you truly love is a fight."

"That's not what this is about."

"Isn't it?"

He sighs, and then the door chimes, and I know he's left the room.

I feel empty and hollow and alone.

24

ALYVOS

*M*y pod's drifted about half the distance toward the enemy barge when I realize I don't want to do this.

I've been waiting for the eagerness to sweep through me, the same hot, hungry need for a fight I always get when I'm heading toward a battle. For it to take over me and fuel me with that wild delight I get when there's a rumble to be had. Instead, I've got nothing but an ache in my gut.

I've disappointed Iris. She wanted me to be better than I am. I left the bed of the female I love for vengeance...and I'm not even sure I want it anymore.

Oh, I still want it for her. But it's clear that she doesn't agree and she views this as a betrayal. So as my pod drifts through the stars, heading on a slow course toward the glitzy barge on the other side of the moon, I wonder if I've keffed up everything in my life.

Is she right? Am I so attuned to wanting to fight that I choose it over everything? If Iris doesn't want revenge, how can I want it for her? The thought gnaws at me as the pod drifts and drifts. I know it'll take forever to get there. I've done this before, a half-dozen times easily. I'm cut off from the others comm-wise because the pod has to be powered down to fly under the barge's radars. Normally I relax until I arrive, or mentally run through battles to prep myself. A few times, I've slept.

Today, though, all I can think about is Iris. Iris and the soft gasps she made when I was so deep inside her, the look on her face when my spur grazed against her clit. The clench of her cunt around my cock and the way she tasted. She was perfection.

And I left that behind.

I bite back a groan.

If you want to hit something more than you want me, then go.

I'd dismissed her words, but now I'm not so sure she was wrong. I told her before that I was broken, and I don't expect to change. But maybe I should try harder to be the male she needs instead of the male that I am. Maybe I should think beyond my fists. Try to solve this without needing a fight. Do this right.

Prove to Iris that I'm more than a pair of fists.

I think of how she'd let the blankets slide down to her waist, exposing those deliciously rounded breasts of hers. Can I entice you to stay?

Keffing fool that I am, I said no. I'm the worst kind of idiot.

The pod drifts, and as it does, I see the barge in the distance. On the dashboard of the pod, in reach, is the disabler. I need to attach that to the underside panel, right where the engine is. It'll mask my own life-support signs as well as scramble the engine signals of the barge. Their ship will be temporarily disabled and we can board.

I'll get the fight I wanted...unless I find another way. There has to be a path that will please Iris and still take down Lord Shitstain.

So I think. And think. It's not my strength. Kivian's the sly brains of the crew. Sentorr'd be great at coming up with a reasonable plan. Me and Tarekh are the muscles, and it's hard to try and think of something on my own.

But I want to please Iris. For the first time in my life since the war broke my soul, I want something more than I want the high that comes with a good fight.

I want my female.

25

IRIS

I'm numb as I dress and head onto the bridge. I don't care that I smell like sex or that I'm sweaty and somewhat sticky from my stolen moments with Alyvos. I can't go into the bathroom alone, because the small room reminds me too much of my cage. Not that it matters. Let me stink.

Nothing matters except the fact that Alyvos left me. He chose bloodlust over me. He'd rather risk his life on some stupid crusade for revenge than be with me. I have a gut feeling that if he boards that ship, I'll never see him again. He's going to get killed.

And he's going to leave me all alone in the darkness.

Grief chokes my throat as I feel my way along to his chair on the bridge. I can hear other people moving around, but no one's talking. It's just as well—I'm in no mood to chitchat, and if they're nervous, I don't want to hear about it.

Alyvos has decided that picking a fight matters more to him than me. I have to protect myself and acknowledge that while I love him, I can't stay with someone that I can't trust to choose me first. And that hurts most of all.

I love him so much it's like I've been blinded all over again. Losing my sight made me fragile and brittle, hard but easily broken. Losing him will destroy me.

I've barely turned on the comm bands and put the ear piece to my head when I hear someone gasp. It's Fran.

"He's turning around. Something's wrong."

Dizziness swamps me, and I clutch at the panel in front of me so hard that pain shoots up my arms. "What do you mean, something's wrong?"

There's a pause. "Maybe it's nothing," she says quickly.

I make a frustrated noise in my throat. "Don't hide it from me just because I can't see. I'm an adult. Tell me what's going on." There's a scream building in my throat despite my calmness, and I feel that if it escapes, I'll never be able to stop. I'm picturing all kinds of horrible things, though. Alyvos drifting in an asteroid field, dead. Alyvos choking in the vacuum of space. Alyvos with his hands behind his back, brought onto the enemy barge and then they put his eyes out because he's not very obedient...

"His communications are down still," Sentorr says, and his voice is calm and efficient as always. "He set the displacer and then got back into his pod and turned around. He's returning to the *Fool* instead of waiting there for the others. I wouldn't be alarmed just yet."

"This changes things, though," Cat says worriedly. "Do we approach anyhow? Continue forward? Or do we stop and wait for him?"

"We wait," Kivian says. "If there's a problem with going forward, I trust Alyvos to know it. We'll follow his lead."

I hold my breath and put my ear piece back in place, my hands trembling. I'm trying to be calm, but I feel like shattering. I'm barely holding it together, and the sob in my throat is screaming to break free. But I only put on the ear piece and listen to the bands, scanning through them in the vain hope that I'll hear Alyvos's rich voice come over the airwaves. That he'll laugh and I'll be angry with him for a flash and then everything will be okay as long as he kisses me again.

But I hear nothing over the airwaves. Just the same inane, pointless chatter as ever. No Alyvos. Frantic, I flip channels. Once, then twice. Again and again. Over and over, I flick through each band, listening to a few moments of conversation before acknowledging that it's not my alien and then I move on.

I need to hear him speak. I'm desperate for it.

"Pod re-docking to the *Fool*," Sentorr says, his calm voice cutting through my wild thoughts. "Alyvos confirmed on board and all vitals good."

I rush out of the bridge and toward the back halls of the ship, where the pods reattach. There's a series of doors there, and I don't know which one will be his, or even if I'm feeling along the right door. I could be frantically staring down a closet, after all, and I'd never know. But I have to be here when he comes on board. I have to. I bang into one of the walls as I turn a corner and jam my wrist, but I don't care. I'm so full of frantic worry that I barely feel it.

Strong hands grab my arm just as I hear a door slide open. "Careful there, love," Alyvos says, and his voice is like cool water poured over my fried nerves.

I burst into sobs and fling my arms around his neck.

"I'm here," he whispers in my ear. His hand strokes my back. "I'm here, and I was wrong. I shouldn't have left you. You were right to tell me that I was being an idiot."

"I didn't say that," I manage between choked sobs. "Never called you an idiot." I bury my face against his collar, breathing in his scent. Under the familiar, lovely smell of him, there's still a musky hint of sex, and it fills me with longing.

"You sure thought it, though." His voice is filled with laughter, even as he strokes my hair away from my face.

I lightly punch his chest, but my hit is ineffectual. I'm not angry anymore. Just the thought of him in danger burned all the frustration away and left me with nothing but relief. "I'm just glad you're safe."

"I thought this was a great plan at first," he tells me, murmuring against the top of my head as he presses his mouth to my hair. "I'd go in, punch some guys, be the big hero. Then I realized it wasn't what you wanted."

"I just want you," I whisper, clinging to him.

"I know. I wanted you to want more. Then I realized the reason why you were upset. You were scared of being left alone again. And I realized what a keffing idiot I am because if anything happened to me, I can't protect you. And it made me realize that rushing in with my fists isn't the smartest plan after all."

I hold him tighter.

"The entire time I was in that pod, I was regretting leaving your side. I should have been in that bed with you, licking your sweet cunt for hours on end. That seemed way more appealing than going after some petty lord who likes to break his toys. Not that I don't want him to get his comeuppance. I'm just starting to think that sometimes it might be smarter if it's not me rushing in at the front."

"So we're just going to let him go?" From behind us, I hear Tarekh. He sounds disgusted.

"Not quite." Alyvos's hand strokes over my back. "I still disabled their engines. Right now they're drifting on a solar current, but when they go to start things up again, they're going to have a nasty surprise. I figured we could drop an anonymous tip to the nearest planet's authorities and let them handle it."

"And not get our hands dirty? Where's the fun in that?" Kivian sounds amused.

"I've got other fun on my mind," Alyvos tells them, and hauls me into his arms as if I weigh nothing. "Send the signal and let's surge away from here. We'll be in my bunk, enjoying the zero-G."

Someone snorts with amusement. I tuck my body against Alyvos's chest and let him carry me away from the others. I'm still shaking with the fear that gripped me, and I clutch a handful of his tunic to anchor myself against him and remind myself that he's here. That Lord Unto isn't going to touch him.

When the door to his room slides shut with a gentle whoosh and we're alone once more, I relax. Just a bit.

"I've never had anyone else to think about," Alyvos tells me as he sets me gently down on the bed. "Well, except for the crew. But they've always encouraged my recklessness. They don't mind that I go in fists swinging. You're the first one that's ever wanted more from me than just my fighting ability."

"You don't give them enough credit," I murmur. "The others are good people. But not every criminal is worth taking on. You can't save the day every time." I find the fasteners on his clothing and activate them. Immediately the fabric loosens under my grip.

"Yes, but I want to save the day for you," he emphasizes, undressing me even as I undress him. We're both on the same page when it comes to this, at least.

"Let him be someone else's problem," I say with a shake of my head. "I want you here with me."

"I can let him go," Alyvos promises and then presses a light kiss to my mouth. "If that's what you want. But I'm a pirate, Iris. I board ships and steal from people. I get into fights. It's what I do. It's what I'm good at. I don't know that I can change."

I shake my head even as I push his tunic off of his body and then run my hands over his exquisitely muscled arms. "I don't want you to change. But right now, I need you more than I need revenge. Maybe that'll change in six months. Maybe a month from now I'll demand that you go after him if the authorities don't. Until then, I need you with me." I slide my hands down his hips and grip his bare buttocks. God, he's sexy. I'm so relieved he's back with me. "Take on all the small-time jobs you want. Just don't take on something where you can get killed just because you want to fight. Please."

"Wise words." He nuzzles my throat and slides a hand between my legs, seeking out my pussy. "I suppose if I need to choose between a fight and mating, I'll choose the mating." Alyvos nips at my jaw. "Especially if you're involved."

I grab a handful of his short hair and yank, hard. "I'd better be the only one involved," I tell him sharply.

My pirate laughs wildly and then pushes me backward onto the bed. "Absolutely. You're the only one I want. That being said...I know you might not want to stay aboard a pirate ship. Not when you could go anywhere. But can this male that thinks with his fists entice you to stay with him? Give him another shot?"

"You can have all the shots you need," I tell him. "I love you."

"Even if I'm broken and think everything can be solved with a fight?" Alyvos kisses me again, and his mouth is hard and desperate on mine. "I'm not always going to think ahead, love. There might be times I kef things up because my first instinct is to charge in. But say you'll love me anyways."

"How could I not?" And maybe my first instinct will still be fear for a long time, but with him at my side, we can balance each other out. "You're everything I've ever wanted. I love you so much."

He's between my thighs in an instant, my hair-pulling inflaming him beyond all control. He palms one of my breasts and then rubs his fingers through my folds until he finds my clit, and rubs it until I shatter mere seconds later.

When he comes inside me, there's no pain. It feels so good that I gasp with the wonder of it. His body feels perfect against mine.

"My love," he murmurs as he thrusts into me. "My sweet Iris. I need you so much."

It doesn't matter that he's broken, or that I am, too. It's okay that we're flawed as long as we find our way together. So I hold on tightly to him and let Alyvos carry me away to my next climax. I'm safe in his arms. Safe with him forever.

EPILOGUE

Months Later

ALYVOS

*I*ris sits in my lap, nibbling on my ear as I stare down at the cards in my hand and try not to be distracted.

Impossible task. I can feel her ass pushing against my thigh—that enticing, tailless ass—and her breast rubs up against my chest as she whispers against my neck. "Nines."

I grunt, because it's either that or moan her name out, and that might make the rest of the room uncomfortable. "Nines."

Across from us, Fran sighs heavily and tosses a pair of nines onto the table. "I swear, I'm not going to play you and Iris anymore. Her memory's better than Kivian's."

My mate just grins and nips at my ear again.

"Queens?" Cat asks when it's her turn.

"Go eat fish," I say triumphantly. I know it's wrong, but it makes my Iris chuckle in that delightful, husky way of hers, and it's worth looking a bit foolish to the others.

"Fran and Tarekh have the queens," Iris murmurs into my ear and adjusts her visor. It took a few months for us to find a black-market visual specialist that would make her a human-sized visor. Bionic implants were suggested, but they're mesakkah sized and not human sized, and until we can find the right person, she's using a radar-sensing visor. It makes her a lot more confident. She doesn't care about the look, she tells me, as much as wandering into the black unknown. I get that, and so I've hung back on the ship with her in a lot of our more recent jobs. That means Cat goes and does cantina duty with Tarekh.

Cat loves cantina duty. And even though I sometimes itch for a fight, I'm learning how to back up Sentorr on the nav panels and some of the bridge duties. Iris told me that it makes Sentorr happy, which seems strange to me because Sentorr practically lives on the bridge. I don't want to take his sense of purpose from him. I have to admit, though, navigating's kind of fun. It's like a puzzle. Granted, I'm not good at puzzles, but I'm learning.

And it lets me keep Iris company. Win-win.

My female's getting more confident with time, though. She's still never eager to leave the ship, but last run, she headed onto the station with me for supplies. And that bland voice of hers is supplanted by her temper more times than not, which pleases me. I'd rather have fiery, slapping and spitting-with-anger Iris than the Iris who has no emotions.

Fiery Iris is quick to suggest we retreat to our bedroom, and I'm always happy to oblige.

As if she can hear my thoughts, my female leans in and sucks on my earlobe, completely distracting me from the card game. My cock grows hard and I do my best to keep my expression blank, but I know I'm failing. Fran's look of amusement tells me that much.

The game goes around the table. Tarekh goes, then Kiv, then Sentorr, who's left the bridge for a time so he can join in the fun. I try to concentrate on my cards, but all I can think about is the delicious female in my lap and wondering how fast I can extract both of us from the group so I can be alone with her.

"It's your turn," Cat says, a little crossly. She doesn't like losing and is glaring at her cards, much to Tarekh's amusement.

"You're supposed to ask for queens," Iris tells me with a little flick of her tongue against my ear. "Ask Fran."

"Queens," I say, choking the words out. My mate's hand has slid below the table and she's cupping my cock through my trou. There's something about card games that makes her frisky.

Fran slaps the two queens down on the table surface with exasperated amusement. "If her memory's this good, she needs to go on the next job with us. Kiv could use her in the cantina instead of me. Between the two of them, they could clean up like crazy."

"No," I say automatically, ever protective of my Iris. She can stay on the ship for as long as she wants. If she never wants to leave it again, that's fine, too.

"Maybe," Iris says to the others. "Let me play with the idea a little."

Before I can show my surprise, Kivian snorts. "Isn't the idea you're playing with there, sweetheart. Have a care for those of us that just ate dinner."

Iris giggles into my ear.

"I eat fish," I tell them, slapping my cards down on the table.

"You mean you fold," Cat corrects me.

"Whatever." I get to my feet, keeping Iris hauled against my front. She's definitely frisky, her arms twining around my neck. "We'll come back later."

"Uh huh," Fran says, and then gives Kivian an affectionate look that says she's thinking the same thing. Cat just gives her mate a slow wink.

I suspect that Sentorr's going to be left holding all the cards very soon.

I carry my mate through the ship and there's never been such a long walk. The moment we're back in our quarters, Iris is tearing at my tunic. "I meant it," she pants, sliding her hands under the fabric. "Next time you guys have a job, I'll go with. I want to try it."

"We'll see." I gently brush her hair back from her face. "I don't want you to do anything you don't want to do."

"I never do," she tells me with a sly grin and cups my cock again. "Guess what I want to do right now?"

"Me?" And when she nods, I grin. Kef, I love this female.

***

AUTHOR'S NOTE

Hello again!

It feels like it's been forever since I last put out a book, but it's really only been like a month. That's forever in Ruby-time, right? At any rate, it's been a crazy spring over in my world, so thank you for all the love and support over on Facebook as I plow my way back into scheduled work.

This novella ran long. Actually, I'm not sure it's really a novella anymore as much as a short novel, but that's all right! I always say that one of the fantastic things about independent publishing is that I can let the story be as long or as short as it needs to be. Naturally when I'm pressed for time, they run long. Naturally. ;)

I hope you enjoyed Alyvos and Iris! I love nothing more than a big protective hero who tries his darnedest to figure out the puzzle that is his heroine. It was challenging to write a visually impaired heroine, because I had to make sure to avoid describing the sense of sight. You'll notice that a lot of her perspective is about sounds and smells and touches. That being said, it's entirely possible that I got something wrong. If so, I sincerely apologize as my intent is always to be inclusive.

Sentorr's story will be coming soon, but not right away. My original schedule was to get Icehome #2 (Veronica's Dragon) out in April, Dragons #5 in May, and then back to IPB in June. Clearly I'm a wee bit off of what I anticipated, but that's still the schedule I'd like to stick to for this summer!

Well, in addition to writing a few other goodies I've got up my sleeve. No details yet, but soon. Sooooooon.

At any rate, Veronica's Dragon is next. May. Promise.

As always, thank you so much for reading. You don't know how much I appreciate having my 'tribe' of people that get my stories and love to hear them. It's the best thing in the world and I'm grateful every day!

<3

Ruby

CORSAIRS!

You've read the others in the series, right?

If not, allow me to convince you. Pirates! Swashbuckling! Human captives rescued by space rogues who are marshmallows for their females! It's all good stuff and it's all available on Kindle Unlimited.

Click on the icon to start with book 1, THE CORSAIR'S CAPTIVE.

A pirate doesn't ask for permission - he takes.

When I see the delicate human female collared and enslaved by the smuggler I'm about to swindle, I do what any male would do.

I take her from him. It's what I do best, after all.

Now Fran's mine, and I'm never giving her up. On board my spaceship, she'll be safe. She'll wear my clothes, eat my food, and sleep in my bed. I'll keep her safe from a galaxy that wishes her harm.

But my sweet Fran wants nothing more than to return to Earth. How can I take her home when she holds my heart in her dainty, five-fingered hands?

This story stands completely alone and is only marginally connected to the *Ice Planet Barbarians* series and *Prison Planet Barbarian*. You do not need to read those books in order to follow this one.

ALSO BY RUBY DIXON

FIREBLOOD DRAGONS

Fire in His Blood

Fire in His Kiss

Fire in His Embrace

Fire in His Fury

ICE PLANET BARBARIANS

Ice Planet Barbarians

Barbarian Alien

Barbarian Lover

Barbarian Mine

Ice Planet Holiday (novella)

Barbarian's Prize

Barbarian's Mate

Having the Barbarian's Baby (short story)

Ice Ice Babies (short story)

Barbarian's Touch

Calm(short story)

Barbarian's Taming

Aftershocks (short story)

Barbarian's Heart

Barbarian's Hope

Barbarian's Choice

Barbarian's Redemption

Barbarian's Lady

Barbarian's Rescue

Barbarian's Tease

The Barbarian Before Christmas (novella)

Barbarian's Beloved

CORSAIRS

THE CORSAIR'S CAPTIVE

IN THE CORSAIR'S BED

ENTICED BY THE CORSAIR

STAND ALONE

PRISON PLANET BARBARIAN

THE ALIEN'S MAIL-ORDER BRIDE

BEAUTY IN AUTUMN

BEDLAM BUTCHERS

Bedlam Butchers, Volumes 1-3: Off Limits, Packing Double, Double Trouble

Bedlam Butchers, Volumes 4-6: Double Down, Double or Nothing, Slow Ride

Double Dare You

BEAR BITES

Shift Out of Luck

Get Your Shift Together

Shift Just Got Real

Does A Bear Shift in the Woods

SHIFT: Five Complete Novellas

WANT MORE?

For more information about upcoming books in the Ice Planet Barbarians, Fireblood Dragons, or any other books by Ruby Dixon, 'like' me on Facebook or subscribe to my new release newsletter. If you want to chat about the books, why not also check out the Blue Barbarian Babes fan group?

Thanks for reading!

<3 Ruby

Made in the USA
Coppell, TX
10 October 2023

22673013R10111